THE SHOOTING SCRIPT

THE AGE OF INNOCENCE

SCREENPLAY AND NOTES BY

MARTIN SCORSESE
AND JAY COCKS

A Newmarket Shooting Script Series Book

NEWMARKET PRESS • NEW YORK

To our parents
—M.S.
—J.C.

96 97 98 99   10 9 8 7 6 5 4 3 2 1

Library of Congress Cataloging-in-Publication Data
Scorsese, Martin.
The age of innocence: the shooting script/screenplay and notes by Martin Scorsese and Jay Cocks.
p. cm. — (A Newmarket Press screenplay)
ISBN 1-55704-254-3 (pbk.)
1. Age of innocence (Motion picture) 2. Wharton, Edith, 1862-1937. Age of innocence. 3. Wharton,
Edith, 1862-1937—Film and video adaptations. I. Cocks, Jay. II. Title. III. Series.
PN1997.A31183S27   1995
791.43' 72—dc20

95-33697
CIP

Quantity Purchases

Companies, professional groups, clubs, and other organizations may qualify for special terms
when ordering quantities of this title. For information, write Special Sales,
Newmarket Press, 18 East 48th Street, New York, NY 10017, or call (212) 832-3575.

Book design by Tania Garcia

Manufactured in the United States of America.

First edition

OTHER NEWMARKET MOVIEBOOKS INCLUDE

The Birdcage: The Shooting Script

A Midwinter's Tale: The Shooting Script

The Shawshank Redemption: The Shooting Script

*The Age of Innocence: A Portrait of the Film Based
on the Novel by Edith Wharton*

The Sense and Sensibility Screenplay & Diaries

Showgirls: Portrait of a Film

*Panther: A Pictorial History of the Black Panthers
and the Story Behind the Film*

*Mary Shelley's Frankenstein: The Classic Tale of
Terror Reborn on Film*

Bram Stoker's Dracula: The Film and the Legend

*Dances with Wolves: The Illustrated
Story of the Epic Film*

*Far and Away: The Illustrated Story of a Journey
from Ireland to America in the 1890s*

Gandhi: A Pictorial Biography

*The Inner Circle: An Inside View of Soviet
Life Under Stalin*

City of Joy: The Illustrated Story of the Film

*Neil Simon's Lost in Yonkers: The Illustrated
Screenplay of the Film*

Last Action Hero: The Official Moviebook

Rapa Nui: The Easter Island Legend on Film

Wyatt Earp: The Film and the Filmmakers

Wyatt Earp's West: Images and Words

CONTENTS

INTRODUCTION

To keep my balance, I had to remember what Marty said: "It's a love story. What's important is the feeling, not the setting. Just nail the emotion and everything else will follow." I didn't forget, but I did get dislocated, even on location. Especially there.

The first day of shooting *The Age of Innocence* was in mid-March, in a wintry field near an old stone house in rural New York. I had some small experience on locations, and had spent a little time around various video monitors, watching scenes on a black-and-white Sony as they played out in front of the movie camera. But I hadn't ever been so close to a movie before, been so much a part of it and had it be, for so long, a part of me, of so much that I dreamed and hoped. And there it was, suddenly in front of my eyes, happening.

I felt, in quick succession, everything I was supposed to: relief, excitement, elation. But then something new came into the mix, gradually at first, then quickly absorbing every other feeling inside itself. It seemed like confusion. And it felt like sadness.

I didn't know where it came from, and I managed, I think, to mask it. But, watching Daniel and Michelle on that monitor screen, hooded from the direct sunlight, I felt not only that we had found something right but that it was over. That we had discovered it, then left it behind before we had a chance to know fully what it was.

It was the monitor. What was a piece of vital utility to Marty and Michael Ballhaus became, to me, an unbidden vehicle into the near future. I wasn't seeing a film beginning on that screen. It was as if I were seeing something that had been finished without me, as if I'd woken from a dream and already forgotten the most glorious parts. The movie had been shot, edited, scored, released to theaters, and then on to video all in one great jump cut. And I'd missed it all.

Television was one of the most important ways Marty and I had gotten used to seeing movies, especially treasured movies, older movies we tried to learn from:

They lived for us on the small, curved glass screen. There they were finished, inflexible, immutable. Movies on television were, for us, the equivalent of going to the library for research. And here, all too suddenly, I saw *The Age of Innocence,* done and, as it were, on the shelf of the past. In order to get my bearings on the movie still at hand, I had to deprogram myself of all the enforced melancholy of these fantasies, turn away from what I knew and whatever I'd expected.

It was then I understood the surprise—and, sometimes, skepticism—which I heard so often whenever, in the early days, the subject of our work on *The Age of Innocence* came up. It was all about dislocation. Marty and I had last worked together on *The Last Temptation of Christ,* as personal and emotional as any movie Marty has made, the closest, I believe, if not to his heart, then to his soul. That movie, with its passionate, obsessive, self-doubting Christ, may have been unorthodox, but it was at least consistent with the sort of risks Marty was used to taking and expected to take. It was also the sort of wild swing that I was believed, by those who knew us both, always to be urging my friend to take: Here, you go fight, I'll hold your coat.

But *Temptation* was one thing, *Age* another. When I was asked initially about the new movie, I expected that people might think we were playing it safe, doing a cakewalk. Instead, there seemed to be an undertow of interrogative doubt in every polite query and comment. I had one vivid preview of this before production began, when I met a literature professor who had gotten hold of our script. "I looked at the two names on the title page, and thought, 'What the hell is this?'" he told me. "One guy I never heard of, and another guy who makes gangster pictures. What do they know about this?" For him we were a Will Elder cartoon from a vintage *Mad:* a couple of low-born types who stomp into the Victorian parlor and blow their noses on the doilies.

Marty remained indifferent to anyone's preconceptions, and untroubled about what we knew going in. It was what we learned, coming out, along with what we felt throughout that he held most important. Movies, for Marty, are an investigation anyway; we could learn what we needed as we got deeper into the work. We had a single charter: "Nail the emotion." This was a love story requiring fineness and finesse, set among the first families and old order of New York. It was not something we were born to, but then, that might be an advantage. We could come to it without an agenda.

Both of us had responded to the quick of Wharton's novel—to the emotion—and not just to the decoration. We could both learn something from adapting such a book—something, for example, about precision of plotting—and, as we did that, lend something of our own. We wanted to bring the novel together with the spirit of the older movies we admired and, sometimes, loved (see the "Sources" section later in this book). If these disparate films shared something in common, it was a spirit of unwavering—indeed, in some cases, headlong—individuality. They were not paralyzed by the pedigree of their sources.

Classics tend to calcify into respectability. After years of academic approval and adaptation to multi-part public television series, an excess of good breeding settles over them like a thick layer of dust. Just as Newland Archer is stifled, then strangled by the strictures of his society, so do adaptations of uppercase literature tend to come gift wrapped in a dramatic gentility that mutes the hard edges of emotion. We wanted to try, anyway, to do something that was closer to the spirit of those honored older movies. We thought, learning from them, we might fashion a way of not only unwrapping the hard edges, but sharpening them so that they stabbed the heart, not just fluttered past it.

Marty knew that the story, evocative of a particular and fascinating time, was not after all peculiar to it. "The setting's important," he said, "only to show why this love is impossible." True, but the setting is seductive. I'd been seduced by it myself, immediately and irrevocably, when my college crony P. F. Kluge had passed the book along with a spare description of its splendors and a simple statement that it contained "one of the great last lines of dialogue." I had tapped the generosity and catholicity of Kluge's taste relentlessly, so I read the book right away. Each chapter flashed in front of me like reels of a film. But when I got around to giving Marty the book some years later, I let him find out about the dialogue himself. I went back to Sources. I held the book in my hand like a talisman and scattered some of those favorite movie titles in the air like motes of gold dust.

After many long years of movie-watching and movie-talking and occasional movie-making between us, Marty knew this was buffs' shorthand, a way to suggest the ambiance and texture of a movie that might come to pass, not its possible stature. We would, if we were lucky, be casing an area we loved, not moving into the neighborhood. So I handed the book over and hoped hard for luck.

Then I waited a while. Marty put the novel on his shelf but put off reading it, as if by instinct, until an incident in his personal life sounded a resonance with Wharton's narrative. Then, all at once, he picked it up and saw it all.

Marty immediately saw those chapter-by-chapter reels, just as I did. And he saw more. He saw scenes. He saw shots. He saw camera moves. And he saw cuts. I think the whole movie was in his head by the time he turned the last page. While we eagerly began to share and explore all the book's possibilities, we also did a little research. We discovered *The Age of Innocence* had been dramatized on Broadway, with Katharine Cornell, in 1928, and subsequently filmed (this was news) as an early talkie with Irene Dunne and John Boles. The film, which we never managed to see, is obscure, but this would not have been a matter of moment to the author. Her interest in movies seems to have been as a marketplace, not as a medium. She sold rights to several of her works, including the short story "The Old Maid," which turned into the immemorial Bette Davis–Miriam Hopkins weepie, and *The Glimpses of the Moon*, a novel that became a silent success with the participation of the stars Bebe Daniels, Nita Naldi, and Maurice Costello, and with the collaboration of F. Scott Fitzgerald, who worked on the script.

Wharton's literary reputation had, over the years, lost some prominence, if not luster. Despite the exemplary efforts of her biographer, R.W. B. Lewis, and others, she was popularly imagined—if she was thought of at all—as a kind of Jamesian acolyte, a monied snob whose best-remembered work (*Ethan Frome*) was her least typical and shortest, known primarily because it showed up on secondary school reading lists. Coming to *Age* was like finding a treasure that had been lost through unfair neglect and misunderstanding. Its story was as vivid as its milieu was tangible. Reading it over repeatedly, scrawling marginal notes, we could feel its melancholy in our shared spirit even as we imagined the plot passing before our eyes, like a brougham emerging from the fog. We hailed the carriage, climbed in, and let it take us away.

Marty, with every new movie, was becoming ever more adept at rendering the shadings and exactitudes of various contemporary subcultures. His fierce eye for detail and his palpable evocation of social nuance would, I thought, have equally dazzling results turned to another time, a less familiar place. Here, I had an insider's edge. I knew my friend was an avid reader of history and was fascinated, as well, with social forms and rituals. This put the New York of Edith Wharton much closer to his hand than most people, who knew him through his work—or thought they did—might realize.

After twenty-two years of friendship, too, Marty and I had enough personal history together—some of it bruising—to have a sense of what lay close to each other's heart. Marty was well aware that I knew something of yearning and commitment, and something more about fear of risk, and loss, and personal havoc. For my own part, I was sure my friend had a clear eye for passion, a soul that, in all important things, was fearless, and a white-knuckle grasp of wayward love. Out of all this, shared and understood, a good movie might be started.

What seemed so obvious to two old friends was not quickly apparent to most anyone else. But we enjoyed taking everyone by surprise, and when the first draft of the script was finished in early February of 1989, after an intense and satisfying three weeks of work, the surprise was suddenly enhanced. To all those who read the script—everyone whose job it is to decide whether to make the film and whether to participate in it—surprise yielded to the attractive idea that this might be a different kind of Scorsese excursion, still personal yet rooted in an unfamiliar milieu, romantic but realistic. To our grateful relief, they began to share the possibility of our dream.

This book will give some sense, we hope, of how the dream worked out. It's our hope that, as you see the film and as you read the script here, you'll be taken up too by the precision of Wharton's narrative and the tangled, troubled essence of these characters whose story, set over a century ago, can still call us back so strongly into a tangible past. Yesteryear—that lovely antique word—should seem no longer ago than yesterday.

Of course, it was a giant step back to yesterday. There were prodigious amounts of research, planning, and designing to be done. And a good deal of additional writing, too. A second draft was finished in early December of 1991, and it was this version that Marty took into rehearsal with the principal actors. More changes were made when those several weeks of rehearsal ended. These usually involved dialogue adjustments, but, in one case, we imported two glistening cameo characters from the novel and gave them their heads for a few pages. These parts were cast but never shot. Because of time and length and the growing, awkward suspicion that their presence, amusing and intriguing as it may have been, was also diversionary, they were eliminated soon after shooting began. With regret.

The version of the script presented here, then, is the shooting script, with a little refurbishing. Some structural changes were made on the set, on the day—including a slippery modification of plot, involving a key and an envelope. These changes have been incorporated here, as have some of the dialogue deletions and emendations made during performance.

The ritual reminder/disclaimer has to be unfurled at this point: This script is not the finished movie. It is the thoroughfare by which the final movie was reached, and being a little longer and more meandering than demanded by strict specs, it is not necessarily the most direct route. We've made liberal use of narration. We both were beguiled by the formal beauty and wit of Wharton's language, its sculpted perfection, and wanted to include as much as possible. Marty was so intent on this that, on the set, he timed camera moves to the narration with hairsbreadth accuracy.

There were also lines of dialogue that seemed, on the page, to be an unfair challenge to the actors: words like "pantalettes," phrases like "draw it mild," that were fairly musty with period flavor but seemed to defy fleet contemporary exposition. Marty decided that they should remain as written, to see how they played. The actors, as it turned out, cherished the language; the confidence they drew from the rhythm and shading of the novel's dialogue seemed to anchor them. Much you will read, though, is still subject to change. As this is being written, film is being edited, the movie is finding its final form, and it is likely that there are things here that will not emerge on screen. We are still, now, in process.

The sections in the book which bracket and—we hope—complement the script should convey a notion, first, of how Edith Wharton's world was re-imagined and made real, and, then, act as an introduction to some of the people who fashioned it from the initial inspiration. We're not trying to lay out, start to finish, every step by which the movie was made. Rather, we're presenting a composite of the whole movie experience, passing along some idea of what struck and inspired all of us, what moved and directed and haunted us, and what helped us. These are images, ideas, fragments of thought that, somehow, made their way into the foundation of the film.

As Marty and I chose the pictures, worked with the layouts and found and fit the fragments of text, this book took on a more personal shading. It became a kind of family album, and, even more, the conclusion of the writing process: tracking back, rediscovering sources, redefining and refining the film on paper one last time before we let go. Even though I was invited to participate in the shooting of the film, and hovered eagerly, daily, over that video monitor, I'm still envious of the fine shaping and surgery that Marty, working with Thelma Schoonmaker, accomplishes with the huge raw celluloid manuscript brought forth after thirteen weeks of photography. Although he enjoys the challenging conviviality of shooting more than he likes to admit, Marty favors editing over all other aspects of filmmaking. "Editing, and writing," he said once. "That's what I like best." Both are actions of tempestuous exploration and refinement, focused and private. I think for Marty they are part of a single sweeping generative process in which the actual shooting becomes a kind of supercharged hiatus, to which I was a privileged participant.

On the best days—and they were numerous—we even lost our distance at the monitor. Marty, Michael Ballhaus, and I became, for the moment, enthusiastic spectators at a movie that seemed to have taken off by spontaneous generation. When the moment in front of us was particularly intense, it took Marty a little longer to call "Cut," and, when he did, you could hear, for a second, the scene's emotion in his voice. When the scene was more relaxed, we could respond accordingly. Watching Michelle arrange roses, the three of us laughed and clapped as the camera tracked around a platform which was circling in the opposite direction. Not missing a move while she spun on the platform, handling the stems with unflustered grace, her accent still in place and staying perfectly in character, Michelle said, "You guys need some popcorn."

It's not only the popcorn that is missing here. There are things I saw every evening in dailies, or in previews of the film-in-progress: the voices and bearing of our wonderful cast; all the tonality of light and camera movement; the rhythm of the edited film, the supportive strength of the music. Still. It is our hope you will find the core of the movie here, just as we searched for it as we wrote, during those first weeks, in Marty's apartment, high above Manhattan, looking out wide windows across the park and the concrete over a New York that was long past innocence.

"It's still out there," he said one day. "Maybe just the ghosts. But it's there." "Ghosts" had been mentioned in the novel, and so they found their way into the narration, by a kind of alchemical assimilation. All the writing would work like that: sudden swoops of inspiration followed by the fortifying dullness of routine. A computer, sternly silent, in one room, Marty and I in another, in as much isolation as can be enforced; talk about old movies; talk about the movie at hand, and not yet on paper; talk. There is no clear division of creative responsibility, except for the fact that I actually flog the keyboard and fret when the computer misbehaves; Marty gets to berate me for my high-tech preoccupations (as handy a work escape as any, and more practical than most) and make more phone calls. We both make the coffee.

Either of us can and might say anything. I can make Marty's visual ideas, detailed verbally in fine detail, work on the page, and also kick in the occasional camera idea; Marty is scrupulous about character behavior and nuance, and, in the case of *Age*, more protective even than I of Wharton's language. We both find ourselves, after a few days, discussing the characters as if they, not the computer, were waiting in the next room.

Marty can also be surprisingly, relentlessly specific, even in the early stages of work: It took us a good while, for example, to work out the servings for the Thanksgiving dinner scene and which character should be saying exactly what as the cranberry sauce is passed and spooned from which damn crystal dish. Then everything, sauce and all, is written down, read, discussed. Then there's more writing—occasionally a good deal more—and finally some initial result, subject to—expected to—change.

Sometimes I'll say, in answer to a casual question, that Marty and I are like musicians who have been playing together for over two decades; we can communicate, as musicians do, in a kind of terse shorthand, then follow and build on each other's solos. But I know, even while I'm saying it, that this is a rather romantic self-portrait, a corrective to that imaginary Will Elder cartoon. Secretly, I think that Marty and I, staring across the sky for inspiration, are really more like a couple of Sahara ostriches.

I doubt that Marty, whose animal obsessions run exclusively to a small white dog who makes a cameo appearance in *Age*, will cotton much to the comparison. But it's said that when thunderclouds appear, these desert ostriches will run, by instinct, toward the lightning. The flash reveals where the quick, intense rain, and the dousing sun that follows, will bring forth green grass to nourish and sustain until the next storm. And so it is, I think, with my friend and me: a couple of nomadic ostriches, hotfooting for the light across the shifting sand.

—J.C.

THE AGE OF INNOCENCE

Jay Cocks
&
Martin Scorsese

1 INT. THEATRE - NIGHT   1

New York in the late 1870s.

A bunch of DAISIES makes a sudden sunburst of BRIGHT
YELLOW. A hand comes into frame, begins to sprinkle PETALS
on the ground. CAMERA tilts down to follow petals and we
see part of a woman's SHOE. It is strangely ornate, like
something from an Arabian Nights fantasy.

As this is happening, we hear a burst of a dramatic music,
and a voice singing an ARIA.

CAMERA pans up from the petals to the extravagantly painted
face of a WOMAN SINGER performing an aria from Faust.

PANNING continues through a series of DISSOLVES gradually
revealing that we are on stage in a theater, the Academy of
Music, in the latter part of the 19th century. The stage
setting-of which we see only small portions-is elaborately
painted. The footlights are CANDLES. Just past them, we see
the orchestra, and past the orchestra, a glimpse of a full
theater, lit by LIMELIGHT.

Continue PANNING and DISSOLVING through a series of EXTREME
CLOSE UPS of DETAILS of period evening wear: high collars,
flowing ties, beautiful beading on dresses, jewelry on
necks and wrists, men's cufflinks against immaculate white
cotton shirts, and shoes...women's heels, men's black
patent leather pumps.

PANNING AND DISSOLVING continues through the theater AUDI-
ENCE, past the slightly shabby red and gold painted BOXES,
ending briefly on the plain red velvet WALL of a box.

NEWLAND ARCHER enters. What we see of him first is the perfect GARDENIA attached to the lapel of his jacket. CAMERA
pans up to his face. He is in his late 20s. Handsome,
assured and guarded. He steps toward the front of the box,
joining the company of several men, including LARRY
LEFFERTS who is approximately Newland's age, and SILLERTON
JACKSON, who is older by a couple of decades.

Newland's move toward the front of the box is covered in
TIGHT SHOTS. We still do not have a full view of the theater, and will not for the rest of this scene.

Lefferts looks at stage through pearl opera glasses. We see
his POV: tight, of the stage, and the singer performing.
FLASH PAN off singer through the audience, moving so fast
it gives an almost kaleidoscopic IMPRESSION of rich fabric
and glittering jewels. Now we're back to Lefferts, who
SWINGS opera glasses away from stage and toward another
box.

                                              (CONTINUED)

1 CONTINUED: 1

He SEES: the figure of a woman entering a box across the
way. Although the woman, silhouetted against candles, is
still indistinct and mysterious to us, he recognizes her
and reacts with controlled surprise.

                    LEFFERTS
          Well.

He hands the glasses to Sillerton Jackson, who looks in the
same direction. Newland watches Jackson, who takes the
glasses away from his eyes after a moment and hands them
back to Lefferts.

                    JACKSON
          I didn't think the Mingotts would have
          tried it on.

The men in the box all stare, then turn away and look back
at the stage: all but Newland. His GLANCE FIXES on the
figure of the WOMAN in the box, who we still do not see
clearly. The conversation of the men in his own box annoys
him, but his face betrays a hint of something more than
irritation. The sight of the WOMAN in the box distracts
him. Affects him.

                    LEFFERTS
          Parading her at the opera like that.
          Sitting her next to May Welland. It's all
          very odd.

                    JACKSON
          Well, she's had such an odd life.

                    LEFFERTS
          Will they even bring her to the Beauforts'
          ball, do you suppose?

                    JACKSON
          If they do, the talk will be of little
          else.

ARCHER LOOKS at his COMPANIONS in the box with just a
suggestion of impatience. Then he TURNS and leaves.

                                                      CUT TO

2 INT. THEATER - NIGHT   2

A corridor, decorated with old prints hung from a red
velvet wall and bright with candlelight.

Archer's POV as he moves quickly down the corridor, past
doors leading to the boxes.

Archer stops at one of the doors and enters purposefully.

                                                        CUT TO

3 INT. THEATER - NIGHT   3

The box which had so interested the men. We see first what
Archer notices: a BOUQUET of lilies-of-the-valley.

TILT UP to the lovely young face of MAY WELLAND as she
turns, smiling, to greet Archer. She is radiant. Archer
smiles back at her, and at her MOTHER, seated beside her.

                         ARCHER
          May. Mrs. Welland. Good evening.

                         MRS. WELLAND
          Newland. You know my niece Countess
          Olenska.

We see the back of the COUNTESS's head, her curly brown
hair held in place around her temples by a narrow band of
diamonds. She turns into close-up: this is clearly the figure who drew the attention of Lefferts and Jackson. She
wears a distinctive blue velvet gown. Her face is unconven-
tional, but it is magic.

Archer bows with the suggestion of reserve. Countess
Olenska replies with a nod.

Newland sits beside May and speaks softly.

                         ARCHER
          I hope you've told Madame Olenska.

                         MAY
                    (teasing)
          What?

                         ARCHER
          That we're engaged. I want everybody to
          know. Let me announce it this evening at
          the ball.

                                                    (CONTINUED)

                              MAY

          If you can persuade Mamma. But why should
          we change what is already settled?

He has no answer for this...no answer, anyway, that is
appropriate for this time and place. May senses his frus-
tration, and adds, smiling...
                              MAY

          But you can tell my cousin yourself. She
          remembers you.

Countess Olenska turns.

                    ELLEN (COUNTESS OLENSKA)

          I remember we played together. Being here
          again makes me remember so much.

She gestures out, and we PAN with her across the regal
gathering: this is the first wide view we have had of the
theater.

                              ELLEN

          I see everybody the same way, dressed in
          knickerbockers and pantalettes.

Archer moves to sit beside her.

                              ELLEN

          You were horrid. You kissed me once behind
          a door. But it was your cousin Vandy, the
          one who never looked at me, I was in love
          with.

Archer is a little taken aback.

                             ARCHER

          Yes, you have been away a very long time.

Camera starts to move in as she raises a large fan of eagle
feathers.

                              ELLEN

          Oh, centuries and centuries. So long I'm
          sure I'm dead and buried, and this dear
          old place is heaven.

                                          FAST CUT TO

4 MAIN TITLES   4

    As they end, the voice of a WOMAN NARRATOR fades up
    and we...

                                       CUT TO

5 INT. THEATER - NIGHT   5

    In another box, the handsome MRS. JULIUS BEAUFORT (REGINA)
    draws her opera cloak about her sculpted shoulders. As she
    does this, and leaves the box, we hear...

                 NARRATOR (V.O.)

        It invariably happened, as everything hap-
        pened in those days, in the same way. As
        usual, Mrs. Julius Beaufort appeared just
        before the Jewel Song and, again as usual,
        rose at the end of the third act and dis-
        appeared. New York then knew that, a half-
        hour later, her annual opera ball would
        begin.

                                         CUT TO

6 EXT. STREET OUTSIDE THEATER (14TH STREET) - NIGHT   6

    A line of carriages drawn up in front of the Academy of
    Music. Mrs. Beaufort climbs in a carriage at the front of
    the line and drives away.

                 NARRATOR (V.O.)

        Carriages waited at the curb for the
        entire performance. It was widely known
        in New York, but never acknowledged, that
        Americans want to get away from amusement
        even more quickly than they want to get
        to it.

                                         CUT TO

7 INT. BALLROOM/BEAUFORT HOUSE - NIGHT   7

    Dark and empty, as it is on every other night of the year.
    CAMERA pulls back from chandelier covered in a bag.

                 NARRATOR (V.O.)

        The Beauforts' house was one of the few in
        New York that possessed a ballroom. Such a
        room, shuttered in darkness three hundred
        and sixty-four days of the year, was felt
        to compensate for whatever was regrettable
        in the Beaufort past. Regina Beaufort came
        from an old South Carolina family, but her
        husband Julius, who passed for an
        Englishman, was known to have dissipated

                                      (CONTINUED)

7 CONTINUED: 7

> NARRATOR (V.O.)(cont'd)
>
> habits, a bitter tongue and mysterious
> antecedents. His marriage assured him a
> social position, but not necessarily
> respect.

Through a series of DISSOLVES, the room suddenly comes to
life. Gilt chairs are set out. The chandelier blazes with
candlelight. An orchestra plays. Dancers swoop by.

CAMERA tracks quickly along the carpet as people walk by,
stopping at the front door. TILT UP from feet of an arriving guest: Newland Archer hands his opera cape to a servant
and walks straight into large CLOSE-UP, which blacks out
the camera.

                                                          CUT TO

8 INT. HALL, STAIRS AND DRAWING ROOMS/BEAUFORT HOUSE   8

Archer hands his cape and hat to a servant, greets another
guest and accepts several pair of dancing gloves, which
rest on a table, each set identified with its own handwritten name card. CAMERA stays with Archer as he climbs the
stairs...

...greets Regina Beaufort, who stands at the top of the
stairs beneath an ornately-framed portrait of herself...

...and through the first drawing room, which is SEA-GREEN.

> NARRATOR (V.O.)
>
> The house had been boldly planned. Instead
> of squeezing through a narrow passage to
> get to the ballroom one marched solemnly
> down a vista of enfiladed drawing
> rooms...

CAMERA TRACKS with ARCHER, SNAKING AROUND to show him NOW
in PROFILE, NOW AGAIN from the back, REVEALING details
of the room and OTHER GUESTS moving through the opulent
interior.

> NARRATOR (V.O.)
>
> ...seeing from afar the many-candled
> lusters reflected in the polished
> parquetry and beyond that the depths
> of a conservatory...

CAMERA still TRACKS with ARCHER, MOVING all around him,
as he ENTERS the SECOND DRAWING ROOM, which is CRIMSON.

                                                    (CONTINUED)

8 CONTINUED: 8

                              NARRATOR (V.O.)

          ...where camellias and tree ferns arched
          their costly foliage over seats of black
          and gold bamboo. But only by actually
          passing through the crimson drawing room
          could one see "Return of Spring," the
          much-discussed nude by Bouguereau, which
          Beaufort had had the audacity to hang in
          plain sight.

CAMERA PANS OFF Archer, onto the voluptuous Bouguereau can-
vas, then BACK to ARCHER as he slows his step to take it in
while still proceeding to the door of...the THIRD DRAWING
ROOM. He crosses the threshold and starts across the room
toward the ballroom.

                              NARRATOR (V.O.)

          Archer had not gone back to his club after
          the Opera, as young men usually did, but
          had walked for some distance up Fifth
          Avenue before turning back in the direc-
          tion of the Beauforts'. He was definitely
          afraid that the family might be going too
          far and would bring the Countess Olenska.
          He was more than ever determined to "see
          the thing through," but he felt less
          chivalrously inclined to defend the
          Countess after their brief talk at the
          opera.

As ARCHER enters the light and movement of the ballroom,
we...

                                                          CUT TO

9 INT. BALLROOM/BEAUFORT HOUSE   9

Start on ARCHER'S POV as he enters the party and merges
with the guests. The first man he sees is Larry Lefferts,
deep in conversation with an attractive young woman.

ANGLE on Lefferts. Action slows (double-framing).

                              NARRATOR (V.O.)

          On the whole, Lawrence Lefferts was the
          foremost authority on "form" in New York.
          On the question of pumps versus patent-
          leather Oxfords, his authority had never
          been disputed.

                                                      (CONTINUED)

9 CONTINUED: 9

Double-framing ends. Resume normal action as Archer's POV
continues through the party. Holding court and amusing a
small group of older women is Sillerton Jackson.

ANGLE on Jackson. Action slows again (double-framing).

> NARRATOR (V.O.)
> Old Mr. Sillerton Jackson was as great an
> authority on "family" as Lawrence Lefferts
> was on "form." In addition to a forest of
> family trees, he carried a register of the
> scandals and mysteries that had smoldered
> under the unruffled surface of society for
> the last fifty years.

Double-framing ends. Resume normal action with Archer's POV
moving through the party. JULIUS BEAUFORT, good-looking
with a hint of flashiness, crosses in front of him, conversing with a guest.

> GUEST
> (in mid-discussion)
> But I didn't see you there this evening.
> Madame Nilsson was in such splendid voice.

> BEAUFORT
> (snide)
> The usual splendor, I'm sure.

ANGLE on Beaufort. Action SLOWS (double-framing)

> NARRATOR (V.O.)
> Julius Beaufort had speedily made a name
> for himself in the world of affairs. His
> secret, all were agreed, was the way he
> carried things off. His social obligations
> and the rumors that perpetually swirled
> around him, all were borne easily before
> him.

Double-framing ends. Resume normal action. CAMERA swings to
another part of the room, concentrating now on May Welland
surrounded by gleeful friends who are obviously reacting to
her engagement announcement.

CAMERA moves into close-up of May. She looks up, smiles,
extends her hand.

9 CONTINUED: (2)   9

Now we see her POV of Archer kissing her hand.

                                                          CUT TO

10 INT. CONSERVATORY/BEAUFORT HOUSE - NIGHT   10

Another room. Behind a tall screen of tree ferns and
camellias, Archer presses May's gloved HAND to his lips.

                    MAY

          You see, I told all my friends. Just as
          you asked.

                    ARCHER

          Yes, I couldn't wait. Only I wish it
          hadn't had to be at a ball.

                    MAY

          Yes, I know. But after all, even here
          we're alone together, aren't we?

                    ARCHER

          Always. The worst of it is...

He TAKES A QUICK LOOK around the room: no one's nearby.

                    ARCHER

          ...that I want to kiss you and I can't.

But he does. He steals a FURTIVE KISS, which pleases and
surprises May. They walk to a sofa, which affords a bit of
privacy, and SIT. In CLOSE-UP, Archer absently breaks off a
piece of lily-of-the-valley from her bouquet.

                    MAY

          Did you tell Ellen, as I asked you?

                    ARCHER

          No. I didn't have the chance after all.

                    MAY

          She's my cousin, if others know before she
          does...It's just that she's been away for
          so long that she's rather sensitive.

                                              (CONTINUED)

10 CONTINUED: 10

                         ARCHER
          Of course I'll tell her, dearest. But I
          haven't seen her yet.

                          MAY
          She decided not to come at the last
          minute.

                         ARCHER
          At the last minute?

                          MAY
          She was afraid her dress wasn't smart
          enough. We all thought it was so lovely,
          but she asked my aunt to take her home.

                         ARCHER
          Oh well.

     He smiles.

                                                       CUT TO

11 INT. BALLROOM/BEAUFORT HOUSE - NIGHT   11

     May smiling back. But now she is moving giddily around the
     ballroom floor, swept up in the rhythm of a waltz. The
     background behind her is a blur.

     REVERSE shot of Archer, swirling along with her, returning
     her smile.

     Now they both join the flow of the other dancers, all
     partners in a great social pageant.

     HIGH OVERHEAD ANGLE, looking down: on the entire ballroom
     below, dancers all turning together in a rhythmic tableaux.

                                                       CUT TO

12 INT. SITTING ROOM - DAY   12

     Waltz music echoes out. We start on a CLOSE-UP of an
     engagement ring: a large thick sapphire set in invisible
     claws. We hear the hearty, admiring voice of Mrs. Manson
     Mingott as we start to DISSOLVE.

                       MRS. MINGOTT
          Very handsome. Very liberal. In my time
          a cameo set in pearls was thought to be
          sufficient.

                                                  (CONTINUED)

DISSOLVE ends on medium-shot of Mrs. Mingott. She is hugely
fat, as vast and august as a natural phenomenon, but her
eyes are vibrant, and miss nothing.

May Welland, Mrs. Welland and Archer sit close by Mrs.
Mingott, whose girth is supported by a careful arrangement
of silk pillows very near a window from which she can
confidently watch society come to call.

> MRS. WELLAND
>
> It's the new setting. Of course it shows
> the stone beautifully, but it looks a
> little bare to old-fashioned eyes.

> MRS. MINGOTT
>
> I hope you don't mean mine, my dear. I
> like all the novelties. But it's the hand
> that sets off the ring, isn't it, my dear
> Mr. Archer? My hands were modeled in Paris
> by the great Roché. He should do May's.

She reaches out for May's hand.

> MRS. MINGOTT
>
> Her hand is tempered. It's these modern
> sports that spread the joints. But the
> skin is white.
>   (staring straight at Archer)
> And when's the wedding to be?

> MRS. WELLAND
>   (a little flustered)
> Oh...

> ARCHER
>   (jumping in)
> As soon as ever it can. If only you'll
> back me up, Mrs. Mingott.

> MRS. WELLAND
>   (recovering)
> We must give them time to know each other
> a little better, mamma.

> MRS. MINGOTT
>
> Know each other? Everybody in New York has
> always known everybody. Don't wait till
> the bubble's off the wine. Marry them

> before Lent. I may catch pneumonia any
> winter now, and I want to give the wedding
> breakfast.

As everyone reacts to Mrs. Mingott's statement with
surprise and (at least in Archer's case) pleasure, SOUND
fades down as they continue to talk and we hear the voice
of the...

                    NARRATOR (V.O.)

> Mrs. Manson Mingott was, of course, the
> first to receive the required betrothal
> visit. Much of New York was already related
> to her, and she knew the remainder by
> marriage or by reputation. Though brown-
> stone was the norm, she lived magisterially
> within a large house of controversial pale
> cream-colored stone, in an inaccessible
> wilderness near the Central Park.

As narration continues, CAMERA moves freely around the
Mingott house, showing us rooms and giving an impression
of secure wealth and unquestioned power.

                    NARRATOR (V.O.)

> The burden of her flesh had long since
> made it impossible for her to go up and
> down stairs. So with characteristic inde-
> pendence she had established herself on
> the ground floor of her house. From her
> sitting room, there was an unexpected
> vista of her bedroom.

CAMERA EXPLORES the unusual geometry of Mrs. Mingott's
living quarters as narration continues.

                    NARRATOR (V.O.)

> Her visitors were startled and fascinated
> by the foreignness of this arrangement,
> which recalled scenes in French fiction.
> This was how women with lovers lived in
> the wicked old societies. But if Mrs.
> Mingott had wanted a lover, the intrepid
> woman would have had him too.

CAMERA now MOVES up a long set of stairs, past a GALLERY of
ornately-framed PICTURES. We DISSOLVE from PAINTING to
PAINTING, and from EXTREME CLOSE-UPS of DETAILS in each,
as narration continues.

                                              (CONTINUED)

>   NARRATOR (V.O.)
>   But she was content, at this moment in her
>   life, simply to sit in a window of her
>   sitting room, waiting calmly for life and
>   fashion to flow northward to her solitary
>   doors, for her patience was equalled by
>   her confidence.

DISSOLVE FROM image in PAINTING to Archer, May and Mrs.
Welland, standing up to say their goodbyes. (Narration
concludes over farewells.)

As they finish speaking, a DOOR OPENS behind them and
CAMERA MOVES IN to show Ellen Olenska and Julius Beaufort
entering, just as the other guests are leaving.

>   MRS. MINGOTT
>   Beaufort! This is a rare favor.

She holds out her hand to Beaufort as the others greet each
other. Beaufort moves toward Mrs. Mingott.

>   BEAUFORT
>   Unnecessarily rare, I'd say. But I met
>   Countess Ellen in Madison Square, and she
>   was good enough to let me walk home with
>   her.

>   MRS. MINGOTT
>   This house will be merrier now that she's
>   here. Push up that tuffet. I want a good
>   gossip.

ARCHER and the WELLAND WOMEN drift out into the hall under
Ellen's guidance, as BEAUFORT remains behind, CONVERSING
with MRS. MINGOTT.

MAY and her MOTHER put on their furs.

ELLEN looks at ARCHER with a faintly questioning smile.

>   ARCHER
>   (laughing shyly)
>   Of course you already know. About May and
>   me. She scolded me for not telling you at
>   the opera.

(CONTINUED)

12 CONTINUED: (4)   12

                              ELLEN
              Of course I know. And I'm so glad. One
              doesn't tell such news first in a crowd.

May and Mrs. Welland are at the door. Ellen holds her hand
out to Archer.

                              ELLEN
              Good-bye. Come and see me some day.

Archer looks at her.
                                                     CUT TO

13 EXT. MINGOTT HOUSE - DAY   13

    As Archer follows May and her mother into their waiting
    carriage.

                         MRS. WELLAND
              It's a mistake for Ellen to be seen parad-
              ing up Fifth Avenue with Julius Beaufort
              at the crowded hour. The very day after
              her arrival...

The carriage pulls away from the curb.
                                                     CUT TO

14 INT. DINING ROOM/ARCHER HOUSE - NIGHT   14

Newland Archer is having dinner with his mother ADELINE,
sister JANEY, and Sillerton Jackson.

Start CLOSE on a piece of meat being probed gently with a
knife and fork as if it were a lab specimen. TILT UP to see
Sillerton Jackson looking at his filet with skepticism and
resignation as we hear...

                         NARRATOR (V.O.)
              Mrs. Archer and her daughter Janey were
              both shy women and shrank from society.
              But they liked to be well informed of its
              doings.

CAMERA pans to Janey and Mrs. Archer as Jackson speaks.

                            JACKSON
                   (in midst of holding forth)
              Certain nuances escape Beaufort.

                                                   (CONTINUED)

14 CONTINUED: 14

> MRS. ARCHER
>
> Oh, necessarily. Beaufort is a vulgar man.

> ARCHER
>
> Nevertheless, no business nuances escape him. Most of New York trusts him with its affairs.

> MRS. ARCHER
>
> My grandfather Newland always used to say to mother, "Don't let that fellow Beaufort be introduced to the girls." But at least he's had the advantage of associating with gentlemen. Even in England, they say. It's all very mysterious.

As dinner conversation continues, SOUND fades down and we hear...

> NARRATOR (V.O.)
>
> As far back as anyone could remember, New York had been divided into two great clans. Among the Mingotts you could dine on canvasback duck, terrapin and vintage wines. At the Archers, you could talk about Alpine scenery and "The Marble Faun" but receive tepid Veuve Cliquot without a year and warmed-up croquettes from Philadelphia.

> JANEY
>
> And the Countess Olenska...was she at the ball too?

> MRS. ARCHER
>
> I appreciate the Mingotts wanting to support her, and have her at the opera. I admire their esprit de corps. But why my son's engagement should be mixed up with that woman's comings and goings I don't see.

> JACKSON
>
> Well, in any case, she was not at the ball.

> MRS. ARCHER
>
> At least she had that decency.

A BUTLER offers mushroom sauce to Jackson, who sniffs

(CONTINUED)

almost imperceptibly and motions the butler away. JACKSON
GLANCES at the PORTRAITS of the Archer family antecedents
on the wall, and FIXES on one of a well-fed, slightly flush
older man. He LOOKS OVER at Archer, who is watching him
with bemused understanding.

                    JACKSON
                 (can't resist)
          Ah, how your grandfather appreciated a
          good meal, Newland.

                    JANEY
          I wonder if she wears a round hat or a
          bonnet in the afternoon. The dress she
          wore to the opera was so plain and flat...

                    MRS. ARCHER
          Yes, I'm sure it was in better taste not
          to go to the ball.

                    ARCHER
          I don't think it was a question of taste,
          mother. May said the countess decided her
          dress wasn't smart enough.

                    MRS. ARCHER
          Poor Ellen. We must always remember what
          an eccentric bringing-up Medora Manson
          gave her. What can you expect of a girl
          who was allowed to wear black satin at her
          coming-out ball?

                    JANEY
          It's odd she should have kept such an ugly
          name as Ellen when she married the Count.
          I should have changed it to Elaine.

                    ARCHER
          Why?

                    JANEY
          I don't know. It sounds more...Polish.

                    MRS. ARCHER
          It certainly sounds more conspicuous. And
          that can hardly be what she wishes.

(CONTINUED)

14 CONTINUED: (3)   14

                         ARCHER
                    (argumentative)
          Why not? Why shouldn't she be conspicuous
          if she chooses? She made an awful marriage,
          but should she hide her head as if it were
          her fault? Should she go slinking around
          as if she'd disgraced herself? She's had
          an unhappy life, but that doesn't make her
          an outcast.

                         JACKSON
          I'm sure that's the line the Mingotts mean
          to take.

                         ARCHER
          I don't have to wait for their cue, if
          that's what you mean, sir.

                         MRS. ARCHER
                    (trying to cool things out)
          I'm told she's looking for a house. She
          means to live here.

                         JANEY
          I hear she means to get a divorce.

                         ARCHER
          I hope she will.

                                              CUT TO

15 INT. STUDY/ARCHER HOUSE - NIGHT   15

     CLOSE on a cigar being passed.

     Jackson accepts the cigar from Archer and both men light up
     after dinner.

                         JACKSON
          There are the rumors, too.

                         ARCHER
          I've heard them. About the secretary?

                                              (CONTINUED)

                         JACKSON

He helped her get away from the husband.
They say the Count kept her practically
a prisoner.

                    (shrugs)

Certainly, the Count had his own way of
life.

                         ARCHER

You knew him?

                         JACKSON

I heard of him at Nice. Handsome, they
say, but eyes with a lot of lashes. When
he wasn't with women he was collecting
china. Paying any price for both, I
understand.

                         ARCHER

Then where's the blame? Any one of us,
under the same circumstances, would have
helped the Countess, just as the secretary
did.

                         JACKSON

He was still helping her a year later,
then, because somebody met them living
together at Lausanne.

                         ARCHER

                  (reddening slightly)

Living together? Well why not? Who has the
right to make her life over if she hasn't?
Why should we bury a woman alive if her
husband prefers to live with whores?

                         JACKSON

Oh, it's hardly a question of entombment.
The Countess is here, after all. Or do you
believe that women should share the same
freedoms as men?

                         ARCHER

                  (with some force)

I suppose I do. Yes, I do.

Jackson draws on his cigar.

(CONTINUED)

15 CONTINUED: (2)   15

                              JACKSON
              Well, apparently Count Olenski also takes
              a similarly modern view. I've never heard
              of him lifting a finger to get his wife
              back.

                                                          CUT TO

16 MONTAGE   16

      Of heavy vellum ENVELOPES, written in beautiful calligra-
      phy, being passed from hand to hand and delivered on SILVER
      PLATES; of INVITATIONS being drawn from the envelopes.

                              NARRATOR (V.O.)
              Three days later, the unthinkable hap-
              pened. Mrs. Manson Mingott sent out invi-
              tations summoning everyone to a "formal
              dinner." Such an occasion demanded the
              most careful consideration. It required
              the appropriate plate...

      WE SEE MRS. MINGOTT with members of her HOUSEKEEPING STAFF,
      selecting china and silver from FOLIOS: large leather
      binders filled with sketches of plates, glasses, bowls,
      dishes, serving utensils and silver.

                              NARRATOR (V.O.)
              It also called for three extra footmen,
              two dishes for each course and a Roman
              punch in the middle.

      As these items are mentioned, we SEE THEM in the montage:
      the FOOTMEN; the fancy FOOD; the brimming bowl of PUNCH;
      KITCHEN STAFF busily preparing a feast.

                              NARRATOR (V.O.)
              The dinner, New York read on the invita-
              tion, was "to meet the Countess Olenska."
              And New York declined.

      MONTAGE ends on image of the KITCHEN STAFF DISSOLVING away,
      leaving the kitchen empty.

                                                          CUT TO

17 INT. DRAWING ROOM/ARCHER HOUSE - DAY   17

      Mrs. Archer angrily detailing the slight to the family as
      Janey and Archer attend her.

                                                          (CONTINUED)

17 CONTINUED: 17

> MRS. ARCHER
>
> "Regret." "Unable to accept." Without a
> single explanation or excuse. Even some
> of our own. No one even cares enough to
> conceal their feeling about the Countess.
> This is a disgrace. For our whole family.
> And an awful blow to Catherine Mingott.

Archer is seen now in CLOSE-UP as he watches his mother.
Her voice fades down and we hear...

> NARRATOR (V.O.)
>
> They all lived in a kind of hieroglyphic
> world.

As the narrator speaks, Archer imagines Ellen, seeing her
quickly...

...looking through the cards of refusal. The words loom
large: "Cannot." "Regret." "Must decline." But each of
these rebuffs is sent on a different, luxurious piece of
stationary, each written in a beautiful but strikingly
different hand. She sorts through the invitations, which
FLIP past FAST, like pages in an old flip book. ELLEN'S
face loses its usual composure. Now she turns her head...

> NARRATOR (V.O.)
>
> The real thing was never said or done
> or even thought, but only represented by
> a set of arbitrary signs. These signs
> were not always subtle, and all the more
> significant for that. The refusals were
> more than a simple snubbing. They were an
> eradication.

... and Archer's image of Ellen fades on that last dreadful
word: "eradication."

We are back in the drawing room. Mrs. Archer has reached a
decision and has RISEN from her seat.

> MRS. ARCHER
>
> Don't tell me all this modern newspaper
> rubbish about a New York aristocracy.
> This city has always been a commercial
> community, and there are not more than
> three families in it who can claim an
> aristocratic origin in the real sense of
> the word. Even dear Mr. Welland made his
> money in enterprise. So.
>
> (MORE)

(CONTINUED)

17 CONTINUED: (2)   17

> MRS. ARCHER (cont'd)
> (looking at them with resolution)
> We will take up this matter with the van
> der Luydens.

She starts for the door.

> MRS. ARCHER
> You should come with me, Newland. Louisa
> van der Luyden is fond of you, and of
> course it's on account of May we're doing
> this.

> ARCHER
> Of course.

> MRS. ARCHER
> If we don't all stand together, there'll
> be no such thing as society left.

CUT TO

18 INT. DRAWING ROOM/VAN DER LUYDEN HOUSE - DAY   18

Start on a tight-shot of the patrician Henry van der Luyden
and his wife Louisa. They have the same pale blue eyes,
with the same look of frozen gentleness. They look calmly
at Archer and his mother before them.

> HENRY
> And all this, you think, was due to some
> intentional interference by...

> ARCHER
> ...Larry Lefferts, yes sir. I'm certain of
> it.

> LOUISA
> But why?

We are in a high-ceilinged, white-walled room in the
Madison Avenue house of the van der Luydens. A framed
Gainsborough and a Huntington portrait of Louisa van der
Luyden hang prominently.

> ARCHER
> Well. Excuse me, but...

(CONTINUED)

                    LOUISA

Please, go on.

                    ARCHER

Larry's been going it harder than usual
lately. Some service person in their vil-
lage or someone, and it's getting noticed.
Whenever poor Gertrude Lefferts begins to
suspect something about her husband, Larry
starts making some great diversionary fuss
to show how moral he is. He's simply using
Countess Olenska as a lightning rod.

                    LOUISA

Extraordinary.

                    HENRY

Not at all, my dear, I'm afraid.

                    MRS. ARCHER

We all felt this slight on the Countess
should not pass without consulting you.

                    HENRY

Well, it's the principle that I dislike. I
mean to say, as long as a member of a
well-known family is backed by that
family, it should be considered final.

                    LOUISA

It seems so to me.

                    HENRY

So with Louisa's permission...and with
Catherine Mingott's, of course...we are
giving a little dinner for our cousin the
Duke of St. Austrey, who arrives next week
on the Russia. I'm sure Louisa will be as
glad as I am if Countess Olenska will let
us include her among our guests.

                                              CUT TO

18A INT. HALLWAY AND DRAWING ROOM/VAN DER LUYDEN HOUSE   18A

START on ELLEN'S ungloved HAND as she fastens a bracelet
around her wrist while she walks up the curving marble
stairs toward the closed doors of the drawing room.

18A CONTINUED: 18A

> NARRATOR (V.O.)
>
> The occasion was a solemn one and the
> Countess Olenska arrived rather late. Yet
> she entered without any appearance of
> haste or embarrassment the drawing room in
> which New York's most chosen company was
> somewhat awfully assembled.

SERVANTS open the drawing room doors and ELLEN ENTERS
unhurriedly, still securing her bracelet. Without embarrassment or self-consciousness, she looks back at the judg-
mental faces of New York's elite arrayed before her. Save
for ARCHER, the GUESTS are all older than Ellen by a couple
of decades, and the weight of their judgement hangs heavy
in the air.

HENRY and LOUISA VAN DER LUYDEN come FORWARD simultaneously
and bring ELLEN around the room, making introductions. As
the COUNTESS meets each redoubtable guest, we...

                                                   CUT TO

19 INT. DINING ROOM/VAN DER LUYDEN HOUSE - NIGHT   19

A formidable dinner party is in progress. Start with CLOSE
UP of wine being POURED into glistening crystal decanters
on a sideboard. CAMERA MOVES PAST the decanters to see what
else is on the sideboard: heavy, elegant silver forks,
knives, spoons and other even larger, more formidable
pieces used for serving; delicate glassware; wine coolers
of hand-engraved silver.

> NARRATOR (V.O.)
>
> The van der Luydens stood above all the
> city's families. They dwelled in a kind of
> super-terrestrial twilight, and dining
> with them was at best no light matter.
> Dining there with a Duke who was their
> cousin was almost a religious solemnity.

DISSOLVE to elegant dinnerware on the sideboard, CAMERA
STILL MOVING. As these items are mentioned in the narration, we see DETAILS OF PATTERNS on each, as they DISSOLVE
from one to another while the CAMERA GLIDES past.

> NARRATOR (V.O.)
>
> The Trevenna George II plate was out. So
> was the van der Luyden Lowestoft, from the
> East India Company, and the Dagonet Crown
> Derby.

CUT to a plate of Maine oysters being consumed by a DINNER

                                          (CONTINUED)

19 CONTINUED: 19

GUEST from a delicate majolica plate.

CUT to FOOTMAN, carving fish at the side table.

CUT to a plate of fine du Lac Sevres being placed on the
table in front of another GUEST.

                    NARRATOR (V.O.)
          When the van der Luydens chose, they knew
          how to give a lesson.

CUT to the CENTERPIECE of the dinner table. We DOLLY IN ON
an epergne laden with FLOWERS and CASCADING WATER.

On THE dolly in, MUSIC SWELLS and SOUNDS of DINNER CONVER-
SATION become more prominent.

CUT to EXTREME CLOSE-UP of an individual ICE MOLD on a
guest's plate. (This signifies a change in the dinner
course.)

CUT TO a direct OVERHEAD SHOT of the whole long table in
the grand room.

CUT to a FOUR SHOT of MRS. VAN DER LUYDEN, ARCHER, HIS
MOTHER, AND THE DUKE, a rather taciturn fellow with expan-
sive whiskers, all conversing at the table. The DUKE is
seated to his hostess' immediate right.

WHIP PAN down the table to ELLEN OLENSKA. She is radiant.

Archer looks down the table at her as we...

                                                      CUT TO

20 INT. DRAWING ROOM/ VAN DER LUYDEN HOUSE - NIGHT   20

Crowded with guests, all enjoying themselves.

Archer, seated on a sofa, continues to look at Ellen
Olenska, who is in easy conversation with the Duke across
the room. She seems to have thawed out the visitor a good
deal. As Archer watches, she gets up and starts across
the room.

Archer keeps watching: will she come toward him?

                    NARRATOR (V.O.)
          It was not the custom in New York drawing
          rooms for a lady to get up and walk away
          from one gentleman in order to seek the
          company of another.

                                              (CONTINUED)

20 CONTINUED: 20

As Archer watches her progress across the room, she does
seem to be coming right toward him.

> NARRATOR (V.O.)
> But the Countess did not observe this
> rule.

She is next to Archer now, smiling as she sits beside him.

> ELLEN
> I want you to talk to me about May.

> ARCHER
> You knew the Duke before?

> ELLEN
> From Nice. We used to see him every
> winter. He's very fond of gambling and
> used to come to our house a great deal.
> I think he's the dullest man I ever met.

Archer smiles, delighted at her outspokenness.

> ELLEN
> But he's admired here. I suppose he must
> seem the very image of traditional Europe.
> Can I tell you, though...
>   (mock conspiratorial)
> ...what most interests me about New York?
> It's that nothing has to be traditional
> here. All this blind obeying of tradi-
> tion...somebody else's tradition...is
> thoroughly needless. It seems stupid to
> have discovered America only to make it a
> copy of another country. Do you suppose
> Christopher Columbus would have taken all
> that trouble just to go to the opera with
> Larry Lefferts?

> ARCHER
>   (laughs)
> I think if he knew Lefferts was here the
> *Santa Maria* would never have left port.

> ELLEN
> And May. Does she share these views?

(CONTINUED)

                    ARCHER
          If she does, she'd never say so.

                    ELLEN
          Are you very much in love with her?

                    ARCHER
          As much as a man can be.

                    ELLEN
          Do you think there's a limit?

                    ARCHER
          If there is, I haven't found it.

                    ELLEN
          Ah, it's really and truly a romance, then.
          Not in the least arranged.

                    ARCHER
          Have you forgotten? In our country we
          don't allow marriages to be arranged.

                    ELLEN
          Yes, I forgot, I'm sorry, I sometimes make
          these mistakes. I don't always remember
          that everything here is good that
          was...that was bad where I came from.

Her lips tremble. She looks down in her lap, at her FAN of
eagle feathers.

                    ARCHER
          I'm so sorry. But you are among friends
          here, you know.

                    ELLEN
          Yes, I know. That's why I came home.

SHE GLANCES toward the door, where MAY, dressed in a gown
of silver and white, is entering with her mother. Several
men, including the Duke, come up to them. Introductions are
made.

                    ELLEN
          You'll want to be with May.

                                              (CONTINUED)

20 CONTINUED: (3)   20

> ARCHER
>   (looking at the men around May)
>   She's already surrounded. I have so many
>   rivals.

> ELLEN
>   Then stay with me a little longer.

And she TOUCHES his knee lightly with her PLUMED FAN.

> ARCHER
>   Yes.

But they are interrupted by Henry van der Luyden and a
guest.

> HENRY
>   Countess, if I may. Mr. Urban Dagonet.

Ellen smiles and Archer gets up to yield his place. Ellen
holds her hand out to him.

> ELLEN
>   Tomorrow then. After five. I'll expect
>   you.

Archer manages to conceal his surprise.

> ARCHER
>   Tomorrow.

And the Countess turns her attention to van der Luyden
and the guest. As Archer walks away from her, he sees
Larry Lefferts bringing his wife Gertrude over for an
introduction.

Now Louisa van der Luyden falls into step beside Archer.

> LOUISA
>   It was good of you to devote yourself
>   to Madame Olenska so unselfishly, dear
>   Newland. I told Henry he really must
>   rescue you.

She looks around with satisfaction at the glittering
gathering.

(CONTINUED)

20 CONTINUED: (4)   20

>   LOUISA
>   I think I've never seen May looking love-
>   lier. The Duke thinks her the handsomest
>   woman in the room.

He catches May's eye. She is indeed beautiful. They smile
at each other.

>   CUT TO

21 INT. DRAWING ROOM/ELLEN'S HOUSE - DAY   21

Start on a large painting, more daring and more modern than
any art we have seen up to now.

Archer stares at it, a little uncertain, a little puzzled.

Another painting, by a different artist, but much like the
first in its subject matter and the unsettling intensity of
its mood.

Archer looks away from this second painting to some of the
odd bits of furnishing in the room: small slender tables of
dark wood, a stretch of red damask nailed on the discolored
wallpaper, a delicate little Greek bronze.

He hears a noise in the hall. A Sicilian maid walks by the
door. Archer looks at her. The maid speaks no English but
understands his unspoken question.

>   MAID
>   Verra, verra.

"Soon, soon." Archer understands, but this does little to
lessen his impatience.

He hears the sound of a horse moving down the street. He
gets up, moves to the window and parts the curtains.

Looking out, he sees: a compact English BROUGHAM, drawn by
a big roan, stopping at the curb. The carriage door opens
and Julius Beaufort climbs down. He turns, and helps the
Countess out.

As Archer watches, Beaufort, hat in hand, says something to
Ellen. She shakes her head. They shake hands and part.
Beaufort climbs back into the carriage. Ellen comes up her
front steps.

Archer turns away from the window. Ellen comes into the
room, taking off her hat and long cloak as she moves
toward him.

>   (CONTINUED)

> ELLEN
>
> Do you like this odd little house? To me it's like heaven.

> ARCHER
>
> (reaching for the right compliment)
>
> You've arranged it delightfully.

> ELLEN
>
> Yes. Some of the things I managed to bring with me. Little pieces of wreckage. At least it's less gloomy than the van der Luydens', and not so difficult to be alone.

> ARCHER
>
> (smiles)
>
> I'm sure it's often thought the van der Luydens' is gloomy, though I've never heard it said before. But do you really like to be alone?

> ELLEN
>
> As long as my friends keep me from being lonely.

She sits near the fire and motions him to sit in an armchair near where he is standing.

> ELLEN
>
> I see you've already chosen your corner.

As he sits, she folds her arms behind her head and stares at the fire.

> ELLEN
>
> This is the hour I like best, don't you?

> ARCHER
>
> I was afraid you'd forgotten the hour. I'm sure Beaufort can be very intriguing.

> ELLEN
>
> He took me to see some houses. I'm told I must move, even though this street seems perfectly respectable.

(CONTINUED)

                  ARCHER

Yes, but it's not fashionable.

                  ELLEN

Is fashion such a serious consideration?

                  ARCHER

Among people who have nothing more serious
to consider.

                  ELLEN

And how would these people consider my
street?

                  ARCHER
           (lightly, disparagingly)

Oh, well, fleetingly, I'm afraid. Look at
your neighbors. Dressmakers. Bird
stuffers. Cafe owners.

                  ELLEN
           (smiling)

I'll count on you to always let me know
about such important things.

The maid enters with a tray of tea, which she sets in front
of Ellen.

                  ARCHER

The van der Luydens do nothing by halves.
All New York laid itself out for you last
night.

                  ELLEN

It was so kind. Such a nice party.

She busies herself with serving the tea. Archer wants
to impress on her the importance of the van der Luydens'
gesture.

                  ARCHER

The van der Luydens are the most powerful
influence in New York society. And they
receive very seldom, because of cousin
Louisa's health.

                  ELLEN

Perhaps that's the reason then.

(CONTINUED)

> ARCHER

The reason?

> ELLEN

For their influence. They make themselves
so rare.

Her observation intrigues him. She watches him as she hands
him tea. The FIRELIGHT makes her eyes gleam.

> ELLEN

But of course you must tell me.

> ARCHER

No, it's you telling me.

She detaches a small gold cigarette case from one of her
bracelets, holds it out to him. He takes a cigarette and
she removes one for herself before closing the case.

> ELLEN

Then we can both help each other. Just
tell me what to do.

A flame darts from the logs in the fireplace. She bends
over the fire. As Archer watches, she stretches her hand so
close to the flame that it seems a faint halo of light
shines around her fingernails. The firelight turns the dark
hair escaping from her braids to russet and makes her pale
skin even paler.

> ARCHER

There are so many people already to tell
you what to do.

> ELLEN

They're all a little angry with me, I
think. For setting up for myself.

> ARCHER

Still, your family can advise you...show
you the way.

> ELLEN

Is New York such a labyrinth? I thought it
was so straight up and down, like Fifth
Avenue, with all the cross-streets num-
bered and big honest labels on everything.

                         ARCHER
            Everything is labeled. But everybody is
            not.

                         ELLEN
            There are only two people here who make me
            think they can help and understand. You
            and Mr. Beaufort.

                         ARCHER
                    (reacts to mention of Beaufort)
            I understand. Just don't let go of your
            old friends' hands so quickly.

                         ELLEN
            Then I must count on you for warnings,
            too.

                         ARCHER
            All the older women like and admire you.
            They want to help.

                         ELLEN
            Oh, I know, I know. But only if they don't
            hear anything unpleasant. Does no one here
            want to know the truth, Mr. Archer? The
            real loneliness is living among all these
            kind people who only ask you to pretend.

She puts her hands to her face and SOBS. Her shoulders
shake. Archer goes to her quickly, bending over her.

                         ARCHER
            No, no, you musn't. Madame Olenska.

He takes her hands.

                         ARCHER
            Ellen.

This is the first time he's called her by her first name,
and it makes him a little self-conscious. He holds her HAND
and rubs it back and forth, like a child's.

After a moment she draws her hand away and starts to com-
pose herself.

(CONTINUED)

21 CONTINUED: (5)   21

> ELLEN
>
> No one cries here, either? I suppose
> there's no need to.

CUT TO

22 EXT./INT. STREET AND FLORIST - EVENING   22

Walking home from Ellen's along Fifth Avenue, Archer passes
a flower shop. He gets only a few steps beyond it, then
turns and goes back.

Inside the shop, the florist greets him instantly.

> FLORIST
>
> Oh Mr. Archer, good evening. We didn't see
> you this morning, and weren't sure whether
> to send Miss Welland the usual...

> ARCHER
>
> The lilies-of-the-valley, yes. We'd better
> make it a standing order.

He notices a cluster of YELLOW ROSES almost fiery in their
beauty.

> ARCHER
>
> And those roses. I'll give you another
> address.

He draws out a CARD and places it inside an envelope, on
which he starts to write Ellen's name and address. But he
stops. He removes his card and hands the clerk the EMPTY
ENVELOPE with only the name and address on it.

> ARCHER
>
> They'll go at once?

In extreme CLOSE-UP, Archer folds his calling card in two
and places it safely in his pocket.

CUT TO

23 MONTAGE   23

A series of rapidly DISSOLVING images: of the maid's hands
on the yellow roses as they are delivered; of Ellen's more
delicate hands arranging the roses in a vase; of Ellen's
face, looking at roses, turning toward CAMERA.

CUT TO

24 INT. AVIARY - DAY   24

   The WINGS of a BIRD FLY past the CAMERA as Archer and May
walk among the cages.

> MAY
>
> It's wonderful to wake every morning with
> lilies-of-the-valley in my room. It's like
> being with you.

> ARCHER
>
> They came late yesterday, I know. Somehow
> the time got away from me.

> MAY
>
> Still, you always remember.

> ARCHER
>
> I sent some roses to your cousin Ellen,
> too. Was that right?

> MAY
>
> Very right. She didn't mention it at lunch
> today, though. She said she'd gotten won-
> derful orchids from Mr. Beaufort and a
> whole hamper of carnations from Cousin
> Henry van der Luyden. She was so very
> delighted. Don't people send flowers in
> Europe?

   He seems mildly annoyed at this. Suddenly the glorious TAIL
of a PEACOCK spreads across the frame as we...

                                                      CUT TO

25 INT. AVIARY - DAY   25

   As ARCHER and MAY sit on bench among the imposing cages.

> MAY
>
> Well, I know you do consider it a long
> time.

> ARCHER
>
> Very long.

> MAY
>
> But the Chivers were engaged for a year
> and a half. Larry Lefferts and Gertrude
> were engaged for two. I'm sure Mama
> expects something customary.

                                                  (CONTINUED)

25 CONTINUED: 25

> ARCHER
>
> Ever since you were little your parents
> let you have your way. You're almost
> twenty-two. Just tell your mother what
> you want.

> MAY
>
> But that's why it would be so difficult.
> I couldn't refuse her the very last thing
> she'd ever ask of me as a little girl.

> ARCHER
>
> Can't you and I just strike out for
> ourselves, May?

> MAY
>   (laughing lightly)
> Shall we elope?

> ARCHER
>
> If you would.

She TOUCHES his arm.

> MAY
>
> You do love me, Newland. I'm so happy.

> ARCHER
>
> Why not be happier?

> MAY
>
> I couldn't be happier, dearest. Did I tell
> you I showed Ellen the ring you chose? She
> thinks it's the most beautiful setting she
> ever saw. She said there was nothing like
> it in the rue de la Paix.

She hugs his arm.

> MAY
>
> I do love you, Newland. Everything you do
> is so special.

CUT TO

26 INT. DINING ROOM/HOUSE - NIGHT   26

The congenial, slightly florid face of Mr. Letterblair
looks straight into CAMERA.

(CONTINUED)

26 CONTINUED: 26

> LETTERBLAIR
>
> Countess Olenska wants to sue her husband
> for divorce. It's been suggested that she
> means to marry again, although she denies
> it.

Angle on Archer, most uncomfortable.

> ARCHER
>
> I beg your pardon, sir. But because of
> my engagement, perhaps one of the other
> members of our firm could consider the
> matter.

> LETTERBLAIR
>
> But precisely because of your prospective
> alliance...and considering that several
> members of the family have already asked
> for you...I'd like you to consider the
> case.

> ARCHER
>
> It's a family matter. Perhaps it's best
> settled by the family.

> LETTERBLAIR
>
> Oh their position is clear. They are
> entirely, and rightly, against a divorce.
> But Countess Olenska still insists on a
> legal opinion.

                                                            CUT TO

27 INT. DINING ROOM/LETTERBLAIR HOUSE - NIGHT   27

CAMERA follows a bowl of oyster soup as it is being served.

> LETTERBLAIR (V.O.)
>
> But really, what's the use of a divorce?
> She's here, he's there and the whole
> Atlantic's between them.

FAST DISSOLVE to next course being served: shad and
cucumbers.

> LETTERBLAIR (V.O.)
>
> As things go, Olenski's acted generously.
> He's already returned some of her money
> without being asked.

Another FAST DISSOLVE to next course: young broiled turkey
with corn fritters.

                                                       (CONTINUED)

27 CONTINUED: 27

> LETTERBLAIR (V.O.)
> She'll never get a dollar more than that.
> Although I understand she attaches no
> importance to the money, other than the
> support it provides for Medora Manson.

Another FAST DISSOLVE to the final course: canvasback duck
with currant jelly and a celery mayonnaise.

> LETTERBLAIR (V.O.)
> Considering all that, the wisest thing
> really is to do as the family says. Just
> let well enough alone.

Fast PAN up to Archer.

> ARCHER
> I think that's for her to decide.

                                                        CUT TO
28 INT. LIBRARY/LETTERBLAIR HOUSE   28

START on EXTREME CLOSE-UP of an exceptionally fine pair of
small GOLD SCISSORS neatly CLIPPING the end of a cigar.

CUT TO CLOSE-UP of the edge of the cigar being LIT.

CUT TO CLOSE-UP of LETTERBLAIR puffing on the cigar.

> LETTERBLAIR
> Have you considered the consequences if
> the Countess decides for divorce?

CUT TO TWO-SHOT of LETTERBLAIR and ARCHER seated comfortably in the library, where a fire is lit.

> ARCHER
> Consequences for the Countess?

> LETTERBLAIR
> For everyone.

> ARCHER
> I don't think the Count's accusations
> amount to anything more than vague
> charges.

> LETTERBLAIR
> It will make for some talk.

                                                    (CONTINUED)

28 CONTINUED: 28

                          ARCHER

          Well I have heard talk about the Countess
          and her secretary. I heard it even before
          I read the legal papers.

                          LETTERBLAIR

          It's certain to be unpleasant.

                          ARCHER

          Unpleasant!

Letterblair looks at him enquiringly and gives him a moment
to calm down.

                          LETTERBLAIR

          Divorce is always unpleasant. Don't you
          agree?

                          ARCHER

          Naturally.

                          LETTERBLAIR

          Then I can count on you. The family can
          count on you. You'll use your influence
          against the divorce?

                          ARCHER

          I can't promise that. Not until I see the
          Countess.

                          LETTERBLAIR

          I don't understand you, Mr. Archer.

Archer reaches into his pocket and pulls out one of his
cards, along with a gold pencil. He starts to write a brief
MESSAGE on the back.

                          LETTERBLAIR

          Do you want to marry into a family with a
          scandalous divorce suit hanging over it?

                          ARCHER

          I don't think that has anything to do with
          the case.

He finishes the note.

                          ARCHER

          Can someone take this for me, please. To
          the Countess.

                                              (CONTINUED)

28 CONTINUED: (2)   28

    CAMERA in close on note, of which we see, in extreme CLOSE-
UP, a few crucial words: "important"; "see"; "soonest."

                                                               CUT TO

29 INT. FOYER/ELLEN'S HOUSE - NIGHT   29

    The maid opens the front door to admit Archer. He enters
and takes off his hat and coat, walking into tight CLOSE-
UP. He spots something in the foyer.

    We see, as he does: on a bench, in the hallway, a sable-
lined overcoat and a folded opera hat. We move closer in a
very fast series of DISSOLVES until we see: the dull silk
LINING of the hat, and the initials J. B. sewn in gold.

    Archer reacts to this, and to voices behind him. He turns,
and sees Ellen coming from the drawing room accompanied by
Julius Beaufort.

                    BEAUFORT
         Three days at Skuytercliff with the van
         der Luydens! You'd better take your fur
         and a hot water bottle.

                    ELLEN
         Is the house that cold?

    She holds her hand out to Archer in greeting as she speaks.

                    BEAUFORT
         No, but Louisa is.

    He nods carelessly at Archer.

                    BEAUFORT
         Join me at Delmonicos Sunday instead.
         I'm having a nice oyster supper, in
         your honor.

    The maid helps him on with his coat.

                    BEAUFORT
         Private room, congenial company. Artists
         and so on.

                    ELLEN
         That's very tempting. I haven't met a
         single artist since I've been here.

                                              (CONTINUED)

29 CONTINUED: 29

> ARCHER
>
> I know one or two painters I could bring
> to see you, if you'd allow me.

> BEAUFORT
>
> Painters? Are there any painters in New
> York?

> ELLEN
>
> (smiling)
>
> Thank you. But I was really thinking of
> singers, actors, musicians. Dramatic
> artists. There were always so many in my
> husband's house.
>
> (to Beaufort)
>
> Can I write tomorrow and let you know?
> It's too late to decide this evening.

> BEAUFORT
>
> Is this late?

> ELLEN
>
> Yes, because I still have to talk business
> with Mr. Archer.

> BEAUFORT
>
> Oh.

He starts to leave, but turns.

> BEAUFORT
>
> Of course, Newland, if you can persuade
> the Countess to change her mind about
> Sunday, you can join us too.

He leaves and the maid closes the door firmly behind him.

                                                          CUT TO

30 INT. DRAWING ROOM/ELLEN'S HOUSE - NIGHT   30

Archer sits close, across from her, in an armchair.

> ELLEN
>
> You know painters, then? You live in their
> milieu?

> ARCHER
>
> Oh, not exactly.

                                                      (CONTINUED)

                              ELLEN

But you care for such things?

                              ARCHER

Immensely. When I'm in Paris or London I
never miss an exhibition. I try to keep
up.

                              ELLEN

I used to care immensely too. My life was
full of such things. But now I want to
cast off all my old life...to become a
complete American and try to be like
everybody else.

                              ARCHER

You'll never be like everybody else.

                              ELLEN

Don't say that to me, please. I just want
to put all the old things behind me.

                              ARCHER

I know. Mr. Letterblair told me.

                              ELLEN

Mr. Letterblair?

                              ARCHER

Yes. I've come because he asked me to. I'm
in the firm.

                              ELLEN

You mean it's you who'll manage everything
for me? I can talk to you? That's so much
easier.

                              ARCHER

Yes ... I'm here to talk about it. I've
read all the legal papers, and the letter
from the Count.

                              ELLEN

It was vile.

He NOTICES her hands, sees she's wearing THREE RINGS on her
third and fourth fingers. But there is no wedding ring. He
says, as he's noticing...

                                                        (CONTINUED)

                         ARCHER (V.O.)
          But if he chooses to fight the case, he
          can say things that might be unpleas...

His glance comes back up to her face.

                           ARCHER
          ...might be disagreeable to you. Say them
          publicly, so that they could be damaging
          even if...

                           ELLEN
          If?

                           ARCHER
          Even if they were unfounded.

                           ELLEN
          What harm could accusations like that do
          me here?

                           ARCHER
          Perhaps more harm than anywhere else. Our
          legislation favors divorce. But our social
          customs don't.

A small travel clock TICKS on the table beside her.

                           ELLEN
          Yes. So my family tells me. Our family.
          You'll be my cousin soon. And you agree
          with them?

                           ARCHER
          If what your husband hints is true, or you
          have no way of disproving it...yes. What
          could you possibly gain that would make up
          for the scandal?

                           ELLEN
          My freedom. Is that nothing?

                           ARCHER
          But aren't you free already?

She looks at him.

30 CONTINUED: (3)   30

                              ARCHER
          It's my business to help you see these
          things just the way the people who are
          fondest of you see them, all your friends
          and relations. If I didn't show you hon-
          estly how they judge such questions, it
          wouldn't be fair of me, would it?

                              ELLEN
          No. It wouldn't be fair.

She looks at the fire. A log breaks in two and sends up a
shower of sparks.

                              ELLEN
          Very well. I'll do as you wish.

He is a little surprised by her sudden agreement. He grabs
her two hands in his.

                              ARCHER
          I do...I do want to help you.

                              ELLEN
          You do help me.

Archer stands up.

                              ELLEN
          Goodnight, cousin.

ARCHER bends to her and KISSES her hands. She draws them
away.

                                                    CUT TO

31 INT. THEATER - NIGHT   31

A production of a vintage play called The Shaughraun. We
see the heavily made-up face of an ACTRESS, at the peak of
a very theatrical moment, resting her arms on a mantle and
bowing her face in her hands. We don't know at first that
we are on stage.

CAMERA pulls out to show actor behind her. He too is very
sad. This is obviously a scene of intense parting.

He moves to a door, then pauses, comes back. While the
actress still has her face averted, he lifts the end of a
velvet ribbon tied around her neck and kisses it.

                                                  (CONTINUED)

31 CONTINUED: 31

Then he leaves and the curtain falls.

Now in CLOSE-UP: Newland Archer, watching the play. He is
very moved.

As lights come up he looks around the theater. The first
person he sees is Ellen Olenska, in a box with some familiar faces: Larry Lefferts and his wife, Mr. and Mrs.
Beaufort, Sillerton Jackson.

CAMERA moves in on Mrs. Beaufort noticing Archer and making
a languid gesture of invitation.

He rises a little reluctantly from his seat and moves out
of frame.

                                                    CUT TO

32 INT. BEAUFORT BOX/THEATER - NIGHT   32

Everyone is chatting as ARCHER enters in the background.

                    LEFFERTS
          It's fascinating. Every season the same
          play, the same scene, the same effect on
          the audience.

Archer is making his greetings in the box. Lefferts turns
to him.

                    LEFFERTS
          Remarkable, isn't it, Newland?

                    ARCHER
          These actors certainly are. They're even
          better than the cast in London.

                    BEAUFORT
          You see this play even when you travel?
          I'd travel to get away from it.

ARCHER seats himself just behind ELLEN while SILLERTON
JACKSON continues to regale REGINA BEAUFORT with details of
the latest social news.

                    JACKSON
          It was a reception at Mrs. Struthers'.
          Held on the Lord's day, but with champagne
          and singing from the tabletops. People say
          there was dancing.

                                                (CONTINUED)

32 CONTINUED: 32

                         REGINA
                    (a bit intrigued)
              A real French Sunday, then.

ELLEN turns to ARCHER and, inclining her head towards the
stage, says in a low voice...

                         ELLEN
              Do you think her lover will send her a box
              of yellow roses tomorrow morning?

                         ARCHER
                    (surprised)
              I was...I was thinking about that, too.
              The farewell scene...

                         ELLEN
              Yes, I know. It touches me as well.

                         ARCHER
              Usually I leave after that scene. To take
              the picture away with me.

She looks down at the mother-of-pearl opera glasses in her
lap.

                         ELLEN
              I had a letter from May. From St.
              Augustine.

                         ARCHER
              They always winter there. Her mother's
              bronchitis.

                         ELLEN
              And what do you do while May is away?

                         ARCHER
                    (a little defensive)
              I do my work.

The LIGHTS start to go down as the audience settles in for
the next act of the play. Ellen looks straight at him,
WHISPERING now.

(CONTINUED)

32 CONTINUED: (2)   32

> ELLEN
>
> I do want you to know. What you advised
> me was right. Things can be so difficult
> sometimes...
>> (beat)
> And I'm so grateful.

The curtain is up as ELLEN TURNS QUICKLY from Archer toward
the stage, raising her OPERA GLASSES to her eyes.

As the new act begins on stage, Archer rises slowly and
leaves the box.

>   CUT TO

33 MONTAGE   33

Series of quickly DISSOLVING scenes as we hear...

> NARRATOR (V.O.)
>
> The next day, Newland Archer searched the
> city in vain for yellow roses.

(Director's note: camera will move always from left to
right in this sequence, with images dissolving into one
another, creating a circular effect.)

Shot of Archer in florist shop DISSOLVES to shot of Archer,
in his office at the law firm, writing a note to Ellen.

> NARRATOR (V.O.)
>
> From his office he sent a note to Madame
> Olenska asking to call that afternoon and
> requesting a reply by messenger.

CAMERA tracks across note and the words "see you as soon
as..."

> NARRATOR (V.O.)
>
> There was no reply that day. Or the next.

Scene DISSOLVES to street outside florist shop. Archer
walks by. There are yellow roses in the window.

> NARRATOR (V.O.)
>
> And when yellow roses were again avail-
> able, Archer passed them by. It was only
> on the third day that he heard from her,
> by post, from the van der Luydens' country
> home.

>   FAST CUT TO

34 EXT. COUNTRY ROAD - DAY   34

A lovely wintery scene. Ellen Olenska, bundled in warm fur,
sits in a sleigh.

CAMERA moves in as she speaks straight to it.

                        ELLEN
        "I ran away the day after I saw you at the
        play, and these kind friends have taken me
        in. I wanted to be quiet and think things
        over. I feel so safe here. I wish..."

                                            FAST CUT TO

35 INSERT   35

These words, in longhand, as they are in the letter. They
fill the screen as she says them: "...that you were with
us."

                        ELLEN (V.O.)
                    (simultaneously)
        "...that you were with us."

                                            FAST CUT TO

36 EXT. COUNTRY ROAD - DAY   36

Ellen, still to CAMERA.

                        ELLEN
        "Yours sincerely..."

                                            FAST CUT TO

37 INT. LAW OFFICE - DAY   37

Archer, with Ellen's letter in front of him, scribbling a
note at the desk. CAMERA moves in on him.

                        NARRATOR (V.O.)
        He had a still outstanding invitation from
        the Lefferts for a weekend on the Hudson
        and he hoped it was not too late to reply.
        Their house was not far from the van der
        Luydens.

                                            CUT TO

38 EXT. COUNTRY ROAD - DAY   38

A snowy landscape under bright sun. A single tree on a rise
near a winding country road. In the distance, we can just
make out A FIGURE IN A RED CLOAK.

                                            (CONTINUED)

38 CONTINUED: 38

Archer moves into frame in CLOSE-UP. Sees the figure far
down the road. He goes out of frame and we DISSOLVE to...

...Ellen, in the red cloak, with her back to us. Archer
enters frame, and she turns.

                         ARCHER
          I came to see what you were running away
          from.

                                             CUT TO

39 EXT. COUNTRY ROAD - DAY   39

Archer and Ellen walking.

                         ELLEN
          I knew you'd come.

                         ARCHER
          That shows you wanted me to.

                         ELLEN
          Cousin May wrote she asked you to take
          care of me.

                         ARCHER
          I didn't need to be asked.

                         ELLEN
          Why? Does that mean I'm so helpless and
          defenseless? Or that women here are so
          blessed they never feel need?

                         ARCHER
          What sort of need?

                         ELLEN
          Please don't ask me. I don't speak your
          language.

They are walking past an old house with squat walls and
small square windows.

                         ELLEN
          Henry left the old Patroon house open for
          me. I wanted to see it.

Ellen has already started up the front stairs of the house.

                                             CUT TO

40 INT. PATROON HOUSE - DAY   40

A big bed of EMBERS gleams in the kitchen chimney under a
hanging iron pot. Archer throws a log on the embers, looks
over to Ellen.

She sits in a rush-bottomed armchair just across the tile
hearth. Her cloak is loose over her shoulders. She SMILES
at him.

                    ARCHER
          When you wrote me, you were unhappy.

                    ELLEN
          Yes. But I can't feel unhappy when you're
          here.

Archer stands near a window, looking out, not quite able to
look at her.

                    ARCHER
          I can't be here long.

                    ELLEN
          I know. But I'm a little impulsive. I live
          in the moment when I'm happy.

                    ARCHER
          Ellen. If you really wanted me to
          come...if I'm really to help you...you
          must tell me what you're running from.

She does not answer. He keeps looking out the window.

Then he feels her, coming up behind him. Her arms are
around his neck, HUGGING him.

He turns...and sees her as she really is, still in the
chair. He looks back out the window. And now he sees...

The FIGURE of a man in a long coat with a heavy fur collar
coming along the path to the house: Julius Beaufort.

                    ARCHER
          Ah!

He laughs. Ellen moves quickly to his side.

Extreme CLOSE-UP: she slips her hand into his.

Then she looks out the window and sees Beaufort. She steps
back, startled.

                                              (CONTINUED)

40 CONTINUED: 40

                              ARCHER

          Is he what you were running from? Or what
          you expected?

                              ELLEN

          I didn't know he was here.

Archer pulls his hand from hers and walks to the front
door, throwing it open. Bright SUNLIGHT rushes into the
room, silhouetting Archer and Ellen, who is a few steps
behind him.

                              ARCHER

          Hello, Beaufort! This way! Madame Olenska
          was expecting you.

Beaufort enters with assurance, addressing his remarks to
Ellen.

                             BEAUFORT

          Well, you certainly led me a bit of a
          chase, making me come all this way just to
          tell you I'd found the perfect little
          house. It's not on the market yet, so you
          must take it at once.

There is a beat of silence, of some fleeting discomfort.
Beaufort finally takes notice of Archer.

                             BEAUFORT

          Well, Archer. Rusticating?

Archer stares back at him without answering. And Ellen
looks at them both. Of the three, only Beaufort seems
untroubled.

                                                        CUT TO

41 INT. STUDY/ARCHER HOUSE - NIGHT   41

Later. Archer is alone in his study, surrounded by books
he's unpacking from a carton.

                           NARRATOR (V.O.)

          That night he did not take the customary
          comfort in his monthly shipment of books
          from London. The taste of the usual was
          like cinders in his mouth, and there were
          moments when he felt as if he were being
          buried alive under his future.

                                                        CUT TO

42 INT. BEDROOM/ELLEN'S HOUSE - NIGHT   42

    Ellen, at a writing table in the bedroom.

    CAMERA moves in on her as she writes hastily.

> ELLEN (V.O.)
>
> "Newland. Come late tomorrow. I must explain to you."

                        CUT TO

43 INT. STUDY/ARCHER HOUSE - NIGHT   43

    CAMERA moves in on Archer, reading Ellen's note.

    He holds it in his lap, on top of an open book.

    CAMERA shoots CLOSE from the side as he CRUMPLES the note and CLOSES the book, allowing a glimpse of the title: a volume of poetry by Rossetti.

                        CUT TO

44 EXT. GARDEN/ST. AUGUSTINE - DAY   44

    A small FIGURE IN A WHITE DRESS in the distance, surrounded by greenery.

    Archer moves into the frame in CLOSE-UP. He sees the figure across the open lawn in front of him. He goes out of frame and we DISSOLVE TO...

    May, in the white dress. Archer enters the frame.

    (This scene should match Archer's meeting Ellen previously.)

    May looks at him, surprised.

> MAY
>
> Newland! Has anything happened?

> ARCHER
>
> Yes. I found I had to see you.

                        CUT TO

45 EXT. GARDEN/ST. AUGUSTINE - DAY   45

    CAMERA moves into tight CLOSE-UP as Archer and May sit on a garden bench. He takes her face in his hands gently and starts to KISS her.

    His gentleness turns more insistent. She responds at first, but then draws back, a little startled.

                       (CONTINUED)

45 CONTINUED: 45

>   ARCHER

What is it?

>   MAY

Nothing.

They are both a little embarrassed. She lets her hand slip
out of his.

>   ARCHER

Tell me what you do all day.

>   MAY
>   (brightening)

Well, there are a few very pleasant people
from Philadelphia and Baltimore who were
picnicking at the inn. The Merrys are
planning to lay out a lawn tennis court...

CAMERA moves in very close on Archer. May's voice fades and
MUSIC comes up as he stares ahead, not listening to her
litany of daily routine.

MUSIC fades and, quietly, he interrupts her.

>   ARCHER

But I thought...I came here because I
thought I could persuade you to break away
from all that. To advance our engagement.

He reaches for her hand.

>   ARCHER

Don't you understand how much I want
to marry you? Why should we dream away
another year?

>   MAY

I'm not sure I do understand. Is it
because you're not certain of still
feeling the same way about me?

Archer is on his feet.

>   ARCHER

God, I...maybe...I don't know.

>   (CONTINUED)

45 CONTINUED: (2)   45

> MAY
>
> Is there someone else?

> ARCHER
>
> Someone else? Between you and me?

> MAY
>
> Let's talk frankly, Newland. Sometimes
> I've felt a difference in you, especially
> since our engagement.

He starts to protest. She hurries on.

> MAY
>
> If it's untrue, then it won't hurt to talk
> about it. And if it's true...why shouldn't
> we talk about it now? You might have made
> a mistake.

Archer stares at the path. There is a pattern of sunny
leaves beneath his feet.

> ARCHER
>
> If I'd made some sort of mistake, would
> I be down here asking you to hurry our
> marriage?

> MAY
>
> I don't know. You might. It would be one
> way to settle the question.

He sees: under the brim of her straw hat, her face
TREMBLING.

> MAY
>
> At Newport, two years ago, before we
> were...promised...everyone said there
> was...someone else for you. I even saw you
> sitting together with her once, I think.
> On a verandah, at a dance. When she came
> back into the house, her face was sad, and
> I felt sorry for her. Even after, when we
> were engaged, I could see how she looked.

He looks up quickly. There is a look of relief on his face
which he manages to conceal at once.

(CONTINUED)

ARCHER

Is that what you've been concerned about?
That's long past.

MAY

Then is there something else?

ARCHER

Of course not.

MAY

(rushing on)

Whatever it may have been, Newland, I
couldn't have my happiness made out of a
wrong to somebody else. We couldn't build
a life on a foundation like that. If
promises were made...or pledges...if you
said something to the...the person we've
spoken of...if you feel in some way
pledged to her...and there's any way you
can fulfill your pledge...even by her
getting a divorce...Newland, don't give
her up because of me!

Archer is beside her, holding her.

ARCHER

There are no pledges. There are no
promises that matter.

May looks as if a great weight had been taken from her.

ARCHER

That is all I've been trying to say.
There is no one between us, May. There is
nothing between us. That is precisely my
argument for marrying quickly.

She puts her arms around him. He HOLDS her close.

NARRATOR (V.O.)

He could feel her dropping back to
inexpressive girlishness. Her conscience
had been eased of its burden. It was
wonderful, he thought, how such depths
of feeling could co-exist with such an
absence of imagination.

(CONTINUED)

45 CONTINUED: (4)   45

He kisses her again. But more politely.

                                                        CUT TO

46 INT. DRAWING ROOM/MRS. MINGOTT'S HOUSE - DAY   46

ARCHER and MRS. MINGOTT are having tea and talking.

                    MRS. MINGOTT
          And did you succeed?

                    ARCHER
          No. But I'd still like to be married in
          April. With your help.

                    MRS. MINGOTT
          Well, you're seeing the Mingott way. When
          I built this house the family reacted as
          if I was moving to California. Now you're
          challenging everyone.

                    ARCHER
          Is this really so difficult?

                    MRS. MINGOTT
          The entire family is difficult. Not one of
          them wants to be different. And when they
          are different they end up like Ellen's
          parents. Nomads. Continental wanderers. Or
          like dear Medora, dragging Ellen about
          after they died, lavishing her with an
          expensive but incoherent education. Out of
          all of them, I don't believe there's one
          that takes after me but my little Ellen.
                    (smiling)
          You've got a quick eye. Why in the world
          didn't you marry her?

Archer's taken aback momentarily. Then...

                    ARCHER
                    (laughs)
          For one thing, she wasn't there to be
          married.

                    MRS. MINGOTT
          No, to be sure. And she's still not. The
          Count, you know. He's sent a letter.

                                              (CONTINUED)

46 CONTINUED: 46

                         ARCHER
          No, I didn't know.

                         MRS. MINGOTT
          Mr. Letterblair says the Count wants Ellen
          back. On her own terms.

                         ARCHER
          I don't believe it.

                         MRS. MINGOTT
          The Count certainly does not defend
          himself. I will say that. And Ellen would
          be giving up a a great deal to stay here.
          There's her old life. Gardens at Nice with
          terraces of roses. Jewels, of course.
          Music and conversation. She says she goes
          unnoticed in Europe, but I know that her
          portrait has been painted nine times. All
          that, and the remorse of a guilty husband.
          Ellen says she cares for none of it, but
          still. These are things that must be
          weighed.

                         ARCHER
          I would rather see her dead.

                         MRS. MINGOTT
                    (shrewdly)
          Would you? Would you really? We should
          remember marriage is marriage. And Ellen
          is still a wife.

          Behind Mrs. Mingott, doors open and Ellen enters, still
          wearing hat and cloak, her face vivid and happy. She stoops
          to kiss her grandmother and holds her hand out to Archer.

                         MRS. MINGOTT
          Ellen, see who's here.

                         ELLEN
          Yes, I know.
                    (to Archer)
          I went to see your mother to ask where
          you'd gone. Since you never answered my
          note.

                                                      (CONTINUED)

46 CONTINUED: (2)   46

                         MRS. MINGOTT
          Because he was in such a rush to get
          married, I'm sure. Fresh off the train
          and straight here. He wants me to use
          all my influence, just to marry his
          sweetheart sooner.

                         ELLEN
          Well surely, Granny, between us we can
          persuade the Wellands to do as he wishes.

                         MRS. MINGOTT
          There, Newland, you see. Right to the
          quick of the problem. Like me.
                    (to Ellen)
          I told him he should have married you.

                         ELLEN
          And what did he say?

                         MRS. MINGOTT
          Oh, my darling, I leave you to find that
          out.

Archer, who has done his best to abide this teasing, now
rises to go. As he gets to his feet, his hand TOUCHES
Ellen's.

                                              CUT TO

47 INT. MINGOTT HOUSE/DOORWAY - DAY   47

Ellen and Archer at the front door.

We see: extreme CLOSE-UP of their two faces close together,
his mouth near her ear.

                         ARCHER
                       (quietly)
          When can I see you?

                                              CUT TO

47A INT. HALLWAY ELLEN'S HOUSE - EVENING   47A

The SICILIAN MAID opens the door and takes ARCHER's coat.
She hangs it quickly, then PICKS UP a large bouquet of
crimson roses, with purple pansies at their base, and
starts to carry them toward the drawing room.

CAMERA PANS with the MAID and the lavish bouquet as we
hear...

                                              (CONTINUED)

47A CONTINUED: 47A

                          ELLEN (O.S.)
           Natasia, take those to that nice family
           down the street.

Archer turns his attention from the ostentatious flowers to
ELLEN, who's coming down the hall toward him.

                          ELLEN
           And come right back. The Struthers' are
           sending a carriage for me at seven.

She holds out her hand to Archer.

                          ELLEN
           Who's ridiculous enough to send me a
           bouquet? I'm not going to a ball. And
           I'm not engaged.

                                                      CUT TO

48 INT. DRAWING ROOM/ELLEN'S HOUSE - NIGHT   48

Start on CLOSE-UP of Ellen's hand, reaching into a box for
a cigarette and lighting it.

                          ELLEN
           I'm sure Granny must have told you every-
           thing about me.

                          ARCHER
           She did say you were used to all kinds of
           splendors we can't give you here.

ELLEN is standing by the mantle. ARCHER APPROACHES her. We
see his face in the MIRROR, betraying some tangible appre-
hension. Behind him, on a table, is a vase full of orchids.

                          ELLEN
           Well, I'll tell you. In almost everything
           she says there's something true, and some-
           thing untrue. Why? What has she been
           telling you?

                          ARCHER
           I think she believes you might go back to
           your husband.

He is standing close to her. Ellen shakes her head.

                          ARCHER
           I think she believes you might at least
           consider it.

                                              (CONTINUED)

48 CONTINUED: 48

                         ELLEN

A lot of things have been believed of me.
But if she thinks I would consider it,
that also means she would consider it for
me. As Granny is weighing your idea of
advancing the marriage.

                         ARCHER
                    (under pressure)

May and I had a frank talk in Florida.
Probably our first. She wants a long
engagement to give me time...

                         ELLEN

Time to give her up for another woman?

                         ARCHER

If I want to.

                         ELLEN

That's very noble.

                         ARCHER

Yes. But it's ridiculous.

                         ELLEN

Why? Because there is no other woman?

                         ARCHER

No. Because I don't mean to marry anyone
else.

                         ELLEN

This other woman...does she love you, too?

                         ARCHER

There is no other woman. I mean, the
person May was thinking of...was never...

He sees: her hands, holding her fan.

                         ARCHER
                    (slowly)

...she guessed the truth. There is another
woman. But not the one she thinks.

He sits down beside her. He takes her hands, UNCLASPING
them, so her fan falls to the floor.

She gets up and moves away from him.

>   ELLEN
>
> Don't make love to me. Too many people
> have done that.

>   ARCHER
>
> I've never made love to you. But you are
> the woman I would have married if it had
> been possible for either of us.

>   ELLEN
>
> Possible? You can say that when you're the
> one who's made it impossible.

>   ARCHER
>
> I've made it...

>   ELLEN
>
> Isn't it you who made me give up divorcing?
> Didn't you talk to me, here in this room,
> about sacrifice and sparing scandal
> because my family was going to be your
> family? And I did what you asked me. For
> May's sake. And for yours.

She sinks down on the sofa. He stays near the mantle.

>   ARCHER
>
> But there were things in your husband's
> letter...

>   ELLEN
>
> I had nothing to fear from that letter.
> Absolutely nothing. You were just afraid
> of scandal for yourself, and for May.

He puts his face in his hands. After a moment, he goes to
her. She is CRYING like a child.

>   ARCHER
>
> Ellen. No. Nothing's done that can't be
> undone. I'm still free. You can be, too.

Now he's holding her. Her face is so close to his...He
kisses her.

(CONTINUED)

48 CONTINUED: (3)   48

And she kisses him back, PASSIONATELY.

Then she breaks away.

They stare at each other. Then she shakes her head.

> ARCHER
>
> No! Everything is different. Do you see me
> marrying May now?

> ELLEN
>
> Would you ask her that question? Would
> you?

> ARCHER
>
> I have to ask her. It's too late to do
> anything else.

> ELLEN
>
> You say that because it's easy, not
> because it's true.

> ARCHER
>
> This has changed everything.

> ELLEN
>
> No. The good things can't change. All that
> you've done for me, Newland, that I never
> knew. Going to the van der Luydens because
> people refused to meet me. Announcing your
> engagement at the ball so there would be
> two families standing behind me instead
> of one. I never understood how dreadful
> people thought I was.

She SEES him looking at her questioningly.

> ELLEN
>
> Granny blurted it out one day. I was
> stupid, I never thought. New York seemed
> so kind and glad to see me. But there was
> no one as kind as you. They never knew
> what it meant to be tempted. But you
> did. You understood. You hated happiness
> brought by disloyalty and cruelty and
> indifference. I'd never known that before,
> and it's better than anything I've known.

She speaks in a very low voice. Suddenly he KNEELS. The TIP
of her SATIN SHOE shows under her dress. He KISSES it.

She bends over him.

(CONTINUED)

ELLEN

Newland. You couldn't be happy if it meant
being cruel. If we act any other way I'll
be making you act against what I love in
you most. And I can't go back to that way
of thinking. Don't you see? I can't love
you unless I give you up.

Archer SPRINGS to his feet.

ARCHER

And Beaufort, with his orchids? Can you
love him?
(furious)
May is ready to give me up!

With a SWEEP of his arm he sends the orchids flying into
the mirror, SPILLING flowers and water everywhere. Ellen is
motionless.

ELLEN

(quietly)
Three days after you pleaded with her to
advance your engagement she will give you
up?

ARCHER

She refused! That gives me the right...

ELLEN

The right? The same kind of ugly right
as my husband claims in his letters?

ARCHER

No, of course not! But if we do this
now...afterward, it will only be worse
for everyone if we...

ELLEN

(almost screaming)
No, no, no!

They look at each other for a moment more. Then Ellen picks
up a bell and rings for the maid.

CAMERA tilts up from spilled flowers on the floor to the
face of the maid as she enters. She carries Ellen's cloak
and hat, and a telegram.

48 CONTINUED: (5)   48

                         ELLEN
          I won't be going out tonight after all.

                         ARCHER
                      (sarcastic)
          Please don't sacrifice. I have no right
          to keep you from your friends.

                         MAID
                      (in Italian)
          This was delivered.

She hands the WIRE to Ellen, who opens the yellow envelope,
looks quickly at the message, then hands it to Archer.

As he takes it, we...
                                                   CUT TO

49 EXT. GARDEN/ST. AUGUSTINE - DAY   49

   May, smiling joyously, speaks in profile as CAMERA MOVES IN
   FROM MEDIUM TO EXTREME CLOSE UP. The light behind and
   around her is INTENSE.
                         MAY
               "Granny's telegram was successful. Papa
               and Mama agreed to marriage after Easter.
               Only a month!"

End on EXTREME CLOSE UP of her LIPS as she recites those
last three words and...

...CUT TO MAY, full-face now in MEDIUM CLOSE UP, speaking
directly to CAMERA as it MOVES QUICKLY in on her.

                         MAY
               "I will telegraph Newland. I'm too
               happy for words and love you dearly.
               Your grateful cousin May."

CAMERA MOVES into her EYES, so CLOSE that, as she starts to
speak her name, the SCREEN WHITES OUT as we...
                                                   CUT TO

50 INT. DRAWING ROOM/ELLEN'S HOUSE - NIGHT   50

   Extreme CLOSE-UP of May's telegram in Newland's hand. He
   crumples it as if that single gesture would annihilate the
   news it contains.

                                              (CONTINUED)

50 CONTINUED: 50

DISSOLVE to CLOSE-UP of his face, desolate, as another images SUPERS IN OF...

CUT TO

51 INT. PHOTOGRAPHER'S STUDIO 51

...MAY's FACE, upside down, smiling formally.

Scene widens as Archer's face dissolves to show MAY, posing in wedding dress, as seen upside down in the VIEWING GLASS of an old camera.

DISSOLVE TO MAY, still posing, as REFLECTED in the brass-encased LENS of the camera.

DISSOLVE TO the PORTRAIT PHOTOGRAPHER, working under the black hood of the camera.

DISSOLVE TO MAY, POSING in the deliberately artificial setting of the photo studio. CAMERA PULLS BACK to reveal the photo studio, then the camera, then the photographer working behind it, and, finally, Archer, waiting at the back of the studio, watching.

                    NARRATOR (V.O.)
          There had been wild rumors, right up to
          the wedding day, that Mrs. Mingott would
          actually attend the ceremony. It was known
          that she had sent a carpenter to measure
          the front pew in case it might be altered
          to accommodate her. But this idea, like
          the great lady herself, proved to be
          unwieldy, and she settled for giving the
          wedding breakfast.

                                              CUT TO

52 INSERT 52

CAMERA moving down a lavish array of wedding gifts: silver bowls and exquisite china and heavy place settings.

                    NARRATOR (V.O.)
          The Countess Olenska sent her regrets—she
          was traveling with an aunt—but gave the
          bride and groom an exquisite piece of old
          lace. Two elderly aunts in Rhinebeck
          offered a honeymoon cottage, and, since
          it was thought "very English" to have a
          country-house on loan, their offer was
          accepted. When the house proved suddenly
          uninhabitable, however, Henry van der
          Luyden stepped in to offer an old cottage
          on his property nearby.

                                              CUT TO

53 INSERT   53

CAMERA moves in on picture of the Patroon house, where
Ellen and Archer had spoken.

> NARRATOR (V.O.)
>
> May accepted the offer as a surprise for
> her husband. She had never seen the house,
> but her cousin Ellen had mentioned it
> once. She had said it was the only house
> in America where she could imagine being
> perfectly happy.

From picture of the house. ...

                                              DISSOLVE TO

54 INSERT   54

...old postcards of London: 19th century streets filled
with carriages; regal figures in high hats and long dresses
enjoying Sunday in Hyde Park; Bond Street crowded with
shoppers.

> NARRATOR (V.O.)
>
> They traveled to the expected places,
> which May had never seen. In London,
> Archer ordered his clothes, and they went
> to the National Gallery, and sometimes to
> the theater.

                                              CUT TO

55 INT. CARRIAGE/STREET - NIGHT   55

May is close to Archer on the seat, holding his arm. She
has a new attitude of easy intimacy with him.

> MAY
>
> I hope I don't look ridiculous. I've never
> dined out in London.

> ARCHER
>
> Englishwomen dress just like everybody
> else in the evening, don't they?

> MAY
>
> How can you even ask that, when they're
> always at the theater in old ball-dresses
> and bare heads.

> ARCHER
>
> Well perhaps they save their new dresses
> for home.

                                              (CONTINUED)

55 CONTINUED: 55

                              MAY
          Then I shouldn't have worn this?

                            ARCHER
          No. You look very fine.
                    (meaning it)
          Quite beautiful.

She smiles...and surprises him with a kiss. He is DELIGHTED.
She pulls away and hugs his arm.

                                                        CUT TO

56 INSERT   56

Old postcards of Paris: Rue Rivoli and the rue de la Paix,
glittering like jewels strung across a city; the Place de
la Concorde, busy with traffic and regal even at midday.

                        NARRATOR (V.O.)
          In Paris, she ordered her clothes. There
          were trunks of dresses from Worth. They
          visited the Tuileries.

                                                        CUT TO

56A INT. SCULPTOR'S STUDIO - DAY   56A

ARCHER watches as the SCULPTOR ROCHÉ models May's folded
hands in marble. May looks up at her husband and smiles.

                        NARRATOR (V.O.)
          Roché modeled May's hands in marble. And
          occasionally they dined out.

                                                        CUT TO

57 INT. DINING ROOM/PARIS HOUSE - NIGHT   57

A small formal dinner. May holding her own nicely, charming
everyone.

CAMERA moves in fast on Archer. He is in conversation with
a fine-boned man whose face is distinguished by a carefully
nurtured mustache.

                        NARRATOR (V.O.)
          Archer had gradually reverted to his old
          inherited ideas about marriage. It was
          less trouble to conform with tradition.

Archer glances away from his dinner companion to look
across the table at the animated May.

                                                        (CONTINUED)

57 CONTINUED: 57

> NARRATOR (V.O.)
>
> There was no use trying to emancipate a
> wife who hadn't the dimmest notion that
> she was not free.

CUT TO

58 INT. CARRIAGE/STREET - NIGHT   58

Archer and May riding home from the dinner.

> ARCHER
>
> We had an awfully good talk. Interesting
> fellow. We talked about books and things.
> I asked him to dinner.

> MAY
>
> The Frenchman? I didn't have much chance
> to talk to him, but wasn't he a little
> common?

> ARCHER
>
> Common? I thought he was clever.

> MAY
>
> I suppose I shouldn't have known if he was
> clever.

> ARCHER
>   (quietly, resigned)
> Then I won't ask him to dine.

> NARRATOR (V.O.)
>
> With a chill he knew that, in future, many
> problems would be solved for him in this
> same way.

CUT TO

59 EXT. STREET/PARIS - NIGHT   59

As their carriage moves away down a boulevard of flickering
lamps.

> NARRATOR (V.O.)
>
> The first six months of marriage were usu-
> ally said to be the hardest, and after
> that, he thought, they would have pretty
> nearly finished polishing down all the
> rough edges. But May's pressure was
> already wearing down the very roughness he
> most wanted to keep.

CUT TO

60 EXT. STREET/PARIS - NIGHT   60

DISSOLVE into the same street, later. It is still and
empty, near dawn. The streetlamps flicker off in the light
of the new day.

                    NARRATOR (V.O.)
        As for the madness with Madame Olenska,
        Archer trained himself to remember it as
        the last of his discarded experiments. She
        remained in his memory simply as the most
        plaintive...

The last flame goes out.

                    NARRATOR (V.O.)
        ...and poignant of a line of ghosts.

On the word ``ghosts,'' we...

                                                        CUT TO

61 EXT. BEAUFORT LAWN/NEWPORT DAY   61

...a close burst of blazing WHITE.

White of summer dresses and crisp suits, punctuating the
GREEN of rolling lawns by the seaside under a bright afternoon sun.

Newport, Rhode Island, a year and a half later. The
spacious lawn of the Beaufort summer ``cottage.''

CAMERA tracks parallel to a row of men and women standing
against a tent, looking out at something we can't yet see.
Their summer clothes are splendid.

CAMERA continues tracking until it comes to a break in the
row: the raised flap of a tent. May walks INTO FRAME, wearing a white dress with a pale green ribbon around her tiny
waist and a wreath of ivy on her hat. As she walks past the
row of people, she comes toward CAMERA into big CLOSE-UP
and we DISSOLVE to...

May, slowly raising a bow and arrow, taking careful aim,
letting go. Her movements have a classic grace.

The crowd applauds appreciatively at her shot, and at her
form. We see a banner announcing ``Newport Archery
Club/August meeting,'' and, in the distance, more spectators
on the verandah of the Beaufort cottage. A small white DOG
dashes across the lawn, pulling its owner by a leash.

                                                    (CONTINUED)

61 CONTINUED: 61

Two of the spectators are Larry Lefferts and Julius
Beaufort, who watch May admiringly. Beaufort has his
customary orchid fixed to the lapel of his jacket.

> LEFFERTS
>
> She's very deft.

> BEAUFORT
>
> Yes. But that's the only kind of target
> she'll ever hit.

Now we see: Archer, a little in front of them. He REACTS
angrily to Beaufort's remark, but says nothing.

Across the lawn, May makes her final bull's-eye. Archer
starts across to join her.

May, flushed and calm, is receiving a winner's PIN from a
club official as a photographer snaps her picture.

She looks up as Archer approaches. They smile at each
other.

> NARRATOR (V.O.)
>
> No one could ever be jealous of May's
> triumphs. She managed to give the feeling
> that she would have been just as serene
> without them.

May takes Archer's arm and they walk across the lawn
together. They come toward CAMERA in possible SLOW MOTION.

> NARRATOR (V.O.)
>
> But what if all her calm, her niceness,
> were just a negation, a curtain dropped in
> front of an emptiness? Archer felt he had
> never yet lifted that curtain.

                                                            CUT TO

62 EXT. NARRAGANSETT AVENUE/NEWPORT - DAY   62

May and Archer in an open carriage. May handles the reins
of the ponies expertly.

> MAY
>
> Has Regina Beaufort been here at all this
> summer?

62 CONTINUED: 62

> ARCHER
>
> I don't know. There's a great deal of
> gossip. I expect Beaufort will bring
> Annie Ring here any day.

> MAY
>
> Not even he would dare that!

> ARCHER
>
> He's reckless in everything. Even his
> railway speculations are turning bad. But
> he just answers every rumor with a fresh
> extravagance.

> MAY
>
> I heard he gave Regina pearls worth half a
> million.

> ARCHER
>
> He had no choice.

                                                  CUT TO

63 INT. MINGOTT HOUSE/NEWPORT - DAY   63

CAMERA close on the pin May won in the archery contest: an
arrow with a diamond tip, pinned to the front of her linen
blouse.

A stout hand runs fingers along the contour of the arrow
and we hear the voice of...

> MRS. MINGOTT
>
> Quite stunning. It's Julius Beaufort who
> donates the club's prizes, isn't it. This
> looks like him. Of course. And it will
> make quite an heirloom, my dear. You
> should leave it to your eldest daughter.

May blushes and Mrs. Mingott pinches her arm teasingly. We
are in the sun-dappled drawing room of the Mingott Newport
cottage. There is a tea service on a table in front of Mrs.
Mingott; the summer heat is not treating her kindly. She
fans herself continuously.

> MRS. MINGOTT
>
> What's the matter, aren't there going to
> be any daughters? Only boys? What, can't I
> say that either? Look at her, blushing!

Archer laughs. Mrs. Mingott smiles and calls out...

                                              (CONTINUED)

63 CONTINUED: 63

                              MRS. MINGOTT
              Ellen! Ellen, are you upstairs?

CAMERA close now on Archer, startled at the name.

                              MRS. MINGOTT
              She's over from Portsmouth, spending the
              day with me. It's such a nuisance. She
              just won't stay in Newport, insists on
              putting up with those...what's their
              name...Blenkers. But I gave up arguing
              with young people about fifty years
              ago...Ellen!

A maid appears.

                              MAID
              I'm sorry, ma'am, Miss Ellen's not in the
              house.

                              MRS. MINGOTT
              She's left?

                              MAID
              I saw her going down the shore path.

Mrs. Mingott turns to Archer.

                              MRS. MINGOTT
              Run down and fetch her, like a good grand-
              son. May can tell me all the gossip about
              Julius Beaufort.

CAMERA close on Archer.

                              MRS. MINGOTT
              Go ahead. I know she'll want to see you
              both.

                                                      CUT TO

64 EXT. SHORE PATH/NEWPORT - DAY   64

The path descends from the bank where the Mingott house is
perched to a walk above the water. Weeping willows are
planted on both sides of the walk. Through their branches
the Lime Rock LIGHTHOUSE is visible.

Archer walks slowly down the path, as if moving toward a
fate he thought was past him.

                                                   (CONTINUED)

64 CONTINUED:

> NARRATOR (V.O.)
>
> He had heard her name often enough during
> the year and a half since they had last
> met. He was even familiar with the main
> incidents of her life. But he heard all
> these accounts with detachment, as if
> listening to reminiscences of someone
> long dead.

The willow-lined walk curves toward the sea, where there is
a small wooden pier ending in a pagoda-like summer house.

> NARRATOR (V.O.)
>
> But the past had come again into the
> present, as in those newly discovered
> caverns in Tuscany, where children had
> lit bunches of straw and seen old images
> staring from the wall.

BRIGHT sunset. The sun splinters in a thousand pieces.
Archer rounds the corner of the path, and sees the pier and
house in front of him. Then he sees: a WOMAN, back to the
shore, leaning against a rail. He stops, unable to go on.
It's ELLEN.

She looks out to sea, at the bay furrowed with yachts and
sailboats and fishing craft.

He does not move. Ellen does not turn.

A sailboat glides through the channel between Lime Rock
lighthouse and the shore.

Still she has not turned.

Archer looks from Ellen to the sailboat, and back again.

> NARRATOR (V.O.)
>
> He gave himself a single chance. She must
> turn before the sailboat crosses the Lime
> Rock light. Then he would go to her.

He looks to the boat. It glides out on the receding tide
between the lighthouse and the shore.

He looks at Ellen: she seems to be drawn into the sunset.

Back to the boat: it PASSES the lighthouse. Water SPARKLES
between its stern and the last reef of the island.

Back to Ellen. She has not turned.

(CONTINUED)

64 CONTINUED: (2)   64

Archer walks away.

As he goes, we can still see Ellen's figure in the
distance. She does not turn.

                                                        CUT TO

65 EXT. MINGOTT HOUSE/ NEWPORT - DUSK   65

Archer and May leave the house and walk toward their
waiting carriage.

                        MAY
          I'm sorry you didn't find her. But I've
          heard she's so changed.

                        ARCHER
          Changed?

                        MAY
          So indifferent to her old friends.
          Summering in Portsmouth, moving to
          Washington. Sometimes I think we've always
          bored her. I wonder if she wouldn't be
          happier with her husband after all.

                        ARCHER
                (laughs)
          I don't think I've ever heard you be cruel
          before.

Archer helps her into the carriage.

                        MAY
          Cruel?

                        ARCHER
          Even demons don't think people are happier
          in hell.

                        MAY
                (placidly)
          Then she shouldn't have married abroad.

She starts to take the reins of the carriage. Archer lifts
them from her.

                        ARCHER
          Let me.

                                                  (CONTINUED)

65 CONTINUED: 65

He reaches over and, in SLIGHT SLOW MOTION, takes the REINS
from her hands as they start away from the house.

                                                    CUT TO

66 INT. WELLAND HOUSE/NEWPORT - MORNING   66

The dining room: the family is having breakfast. Mrs.
Archer and Janey are at the table, as is Mrs. Welland.
May presides over the gathering with practiced ease. The
morning breeze gently lofts the long curtains. CAMERA
makes CIRCULAR TRACK around table as it PANS with the
conversation.

                    MRS. WELLAND
        The Blenkers. A party for the Blenkers?

                    JANEY
        Who are they?

                    MAY
        The Portsmouth people, I think. The ones
        Countess Olenska is staying with.

                    MRS. ARCHER
        "Professor and Mrs. Emerson Sillerton
        request the pleasure...Wednesday afternoon
        club...at 3 0'clock punctually. To meet
        Mrs. and the Misses Blenker. Red Gables,
        Catherine Street."

She looks around the table.

                    MRS. ARCHER
        I don't think we can decline.

                    JANEY
        I don't see why, really. He's an archaeol-
        ogist and he lives here even in winter.
        He's always taking his poor wife to tombs
        in the Yucatan instead of to Paris. He's
        got a house full of long-haired men and
        short-haired women, and...

                    MRS. ARCHER
        And he is Sillerton Jackson's cousin.

                    JANEY
                (chastened)
        Of course.

                                            (CONTINUED)

66 CONTINUED: 66

> MRS. WELLAND
>
> Some of us will have to go.
>
> MAY
>
> I'll go over. And, Janey, why don't you
> come with me. I'm sure Cousin Ellen will
> be there. It will give you a chance to see
> her.
>
> (to Archer)
>
> Newland, you can find some way to spend
> the afternoon, can't you?
>
> ARCHER
>
> Oh I think for a change I'll just save it
> instead of spending it.

He takes the last bite of griddle cakes left on his plate.

> ARCHER
>
> Maybe drive to the farm to see about a new
> horse for the brougham.

                                                        CUT TO

67 EXT. COUNTRY ROAD/NEWPORT - DAY   67

Archer at the reins of the carriage. The day is clear, the
sky a brilliant ultramarine.

He leans a little way out of the carriage to check a name
posted at the front of the lane, then turns the horses in.

We see the name on the post: Blenker.

                                                        CUT TO

68 EXT. DRIVE/BLENKER HOUSE/NEWPORT - DAY   68

In the near distance, an ill-kept house with peeling white
paint.

Closer: a shed for horses. Archer stops and ties up his
team.

Empty and quiet. The click of locusts in the still air.
Archer looks toward the house, sees...

...to its left, a ghostly summer house of trellis-work that
had once been white.

He walks toward the summer house.

As he gets closer, he sees a box garden, and something pink
just beyond it.

                                                   (CONTINUED)

DISSOLVE to tight shot: a pink PARASOL, inside the summer
house.

DISSOLVE to Archer's face, staring at it, almost hypno-
tized. He walks toward the CAMERA. As he blocks it we...

...DISSOLVE again to the parasol. Close on it as Archer's
hand enters the frame to pick it up. CAMERA moves in on his
face as he lifts the handle close to him. It is carved of
rare wood. He smells its scent.

And lifts the handle closer...slowly...to his lips.

SOUND: of soft skirts behind him. We see: Archer's eyes, in
huge CLOSE-UP, closing in anticipation.

CAMERA pulls out as he waits for Ellen's touch. But he
hears only a voice behind him...

                    KATIE BLENKER
          Hello?

His eyes open. He turns and sees...

...Katie Blenker, an adolescent girl with open, friendly
curiosity. She looks, for an instant, familiar: Archer
thinks that he has been surprised by May.

                    KATIE BLENKER
          I'm sorry, did you ring, I've been asleep
          in the hammock...

                    ARCHER
          I didn't mean to disturb you. Are you Miss
          Blenker? I'm Newland Archer.

                    KATIE
          I've heard so much about you.

                    ARCHER
          I came up the island to see about a new
          horse, and I thought I'd call. But the
          house seemed empty...

                    KATIE
          It is empty. They're all at the party. The
          one the Sillertons are giving for us.
          Didn't you know?

He keeps looking at her, not knowing what to say.

                                              (CONTINUED)

68 CONTINUED: (2)   68

                              KATIE

          Everyone's there but me, with my fever,
          and Countess Olenska...oh, you found my
          parasol!

She takes it from his hand.

                              KATIE

          It's my best one. It's from the Cameroons.

                              ARCHER
                        (trying to be casual)
          The Countess was called away?

                              KATIE

          A telegram came from Boston. She said she
          might be gone for two days. I do love the
          way she does her hair, don't you? It
          reminds me of Sir Walter Scott.

CAMERA moves close on Archer. He is struggling with himself.

                              ARCHER
                        (interrupting her)
          You don't know...I'm sorry...I've got to
          be in Boston tomorrow. You wouldn't know
          where she was staying?

                                                         CUT TO

69 EXT. BOSTON COMMON - DAY   69

A sweltering summer day.

CAMERA close on an oil PAINTING of the park scene. It
nicely captures the trees and flowers under shimmering
heat, the summer colors of suits and dresses...and the
figure of a woman, seated mid-perspective, on a bench,
reading a volume of poetry.

DISSOLVE to an even tighter shot of the woman in the
painting. A BRUSH works on her features.

DISSOLVE to Archer, watching the painter. He turns,
squinting into the glare of the morning sun at the woman
seated a little way in front of him on the bench.

FAST PAN over to her. It is Ellen.

                                                         CUT TO

70 EXT. BOSTON COMMON - DAY   70

Ellen looks up. Archer is beside her.

                    ELLEN
                (startled)
        Oh.
                (now smiling)
        Oh.

Without rising, she makes room for him on the bench. He
sits beside her and tries making casual conversation.

                    ARCHER
        I'm here on business. Just got here,
        actually.

He stares at her. Being casual is too difficult.

                    ARCHER
        You're doing your hair differently.

                    ELLEN
        Only because the maid's not with me. She
        stayed back in Portsmouth. I'm only here
        for two days, it didn't seem worth...

                    ARCHER
        You're traveling alone?

                    ELLEN
                (sly)
        Yes. Why, do you think it's a little
        dangerous?

                    ARCHER
                (smiling)
        Well, it's unconventional.

                    ELLEN
        I suppose it is. I hadn't thought of it.
        I've just done something so much more
        unconventional. I've refused to take back
        money that belonged to me.

                    ARCHER
        Someone came with an offer?

She nods.

                                                    (CONTINUED

70 CONTINUED: 70

                              ARCHER
                What were the conditions?

                              ELLEN
                         (simply)
                I refused.

                              ARCHER
                         (pressing)
                Tell me the conditions.

                              ELLEN
                Nothing unbearable, really. Just to sit at
                the head of his table now and then.

Archer chooses his words carefully.

                              ARCHER
                And he wants you back, at any price?

                              ELLEN
                Well, it's a considerable price. At least
                it's considerable for me.

                              ARCHER
                So you came to meet him.

She stares, then laughs suddenly.

                              ELLEN
                My husband? Here? No, of course not. He
                sent someone.

                              ARCHER
                         (very careful now)
                His secretary?

                              ELLEN
                Yes. He's still here, in fact. He insisted
                on waiting. In case I changed my mind.

He is trying to absorb all this.

                              ELLEN
                They told you at the hotel I was here?

He nods, but still says nothing. After a moment...

                                                          (CONTINUED)

70 CONTINUED: (2)   70

                              ELLEN
            You haven't changed, Newland.

    Now he looks straight into her eyes.

                              ARCHER
                           (intense)
            I had changed, till I saw you again.

                              ELLEN
            Please don't.

                              ARCHER
            Just give me the day. I'll say anything
            you like. Or nothing. I won't speak unless
            you tell me to. All I want is some time
            with you. All I want is to listen to you.

    He is so intense Ellen has to look away from him. She takes
    out a small gold-faced watch on an enamel chain.

                              ARCHER
            I want to get you away from that man. Was
            he coming to the hotel?

                              ELLEN
            At eleven. Just in case...

                              ARCHER
            Then we must leave now. It's been a
            hundred years since we've met.

                              ELLEN
            Where will we go?

                              ARCHER
            Where?

    He's stumped: emotion has gotten in the way of foresight.
    He seems addled for a moment. She smiles at him.

                              ELLEN
            Somewhere cool, at any rate.

                              ARCHER
            We'll take the steamboat down to Point
            Arley. There's an inn.

                              ELLEN
            I'll have to leave a note at the hotel.

(CONTINUED)

70 CONTINUED: (3)   70

He pulls a note-case from his pocket, fumbling a little.

> ARCHER
>
> Write it here. I have the paper...you
> see how everything's predestined?...and
> this...have you seen these...the new
> stylographic pen...

He hands her the case and pulls out a fountain pen.

> ARCHER
>
> Just steady the case on your knee, and
> I'll get the pen going in a second...

He bangs the hand holding the pen against the back of the
bench.

> ARCHER
>
> It's like jerking down the mercury in a
> thermometer. Now try.

He hands her the pen and she starts to write a name on an
envelope. EXTREME CLOSE UP, from in front: of her HAND,
with the pen, beginning to write a name, "Riv..."

                                                  MATCH CUT TO

71 EXT. PARKER HOUSE HOTEL/BOSTON - DAY   71

The envelope, sealed now, with a name we can't read.

> ARCHER
>
> Shall I take it in?

> ELLEN
>
> I'll only be a moment.

She disappears through the glazed doors of the hotel.

An Irish woman walks by, selling peaches. Archer declines.

The door of the hotel opens. He turns. A group of men comes
onto the sidewalk and walks away. Archer watches them with
mild interest.

He hears the doors again and looks over. A MAN, dressed in
a distinctly European fashion and looking a little worried,
appears on the sidewalk. He looks around, but does not seem
to notice Archer.

                                                  (CONTINUED)

71 CONTINUED: 71

   Archer sees him, however. Something about his face is
   familiar, but Archer can't quite place it...

   ...and the man is off, down the street.

   SOUND of the hotel doors again. He turns, and Ellen is at
   his side.
                                                      CUT TO

72 INT./EXT. INN - DAY   72

   (POSSIBLE start on MATTE SHOT of white clapboard inn situated on a bluff overlooking the Atlantic, with a ferry boat
   coming toward it.)

   We see out the window of the inn: the BILLOWING WHITE SAIL
   of a small boat. CAMERA pulls back to reveal...

   ...a long wooden verandah overlooking a gentle lawn and the
   Atlantic. ARCHER and ELLEN sit at a table covered with a
   checkered cloth held down from the ocean breezes by a bot-
   tle of pickles at one end and a blueberry pie under a clear
   dish at the other. SOUNDS of a party in the large dining
   room of the inn occasionally interrupt the stillness.

   Ellen looks at the distant sailboat, then turns to Archer.

                        ELLEN
            Why didn't you come down to the beach to
            get me the day I was at Granny's?

                        ARCHER
            Because you didn't turn around. You didn't
            know I was there. I swore I wouldn't call
            you unless you looked around.

                        ELLEN
            But I didn't look around on purpose.

                        ARCHER
            You knew?

                        ELLEN
            I recognized the carriage when you drove
            in. So I went to the beach.

                        ARCHER
            To get as far away from me as you could.

                        ELLEN
            As I could. Yes.

                                              (CONTINUED

72 CONTINUED:

> ARCHER
>
> Well you see, then. It's no use. It's
> better to face each other.

> ELLEN
>
> I only want to be honest with you.

> ARCHER
>
> Honest? Isn't that why you always admired
> Julius Beaufort? He was more honest than
> the rest of us, wasn't he? We've got no
> character, no color, no variety. I wonder
> why you just don't go back to Europe.

> ELLEN
>
> I believe it's because of you.

> ARCHER
>
> Me? I'm the man who married one woman
> because another one told him to.

> ELLEN
>
> You promised not to say those things
> today.

> ARCHER
>
> I can't keep that promise.

> ELLEN
>
> And what about May? What does May feel?
> That's the thing we've always got to think
> of, by your own showing.

> ARCHER
>
> My showing?

> ELLEN
>
> Yes, yours. Otherwise everything you
> taught me would be a sham.

> ARCHER
>
> If you're using my marriage as some
> victory of ours, then there's no reason
> on earth why you shouldn't go back.
>   (looking right at her)
> You gave me my first glimpse of a real
> life. Then you asked me to go on with the
> false one. No one can endure that.

(CONTINUED)

                              ELLEN
              I'm enduring it.

He looks at her.

                              ARCHER
              You too? All this time, you too?

She does not reply.

                              ARCHER
              What's the use? We can't be like this.
              When will you go back?

                              ELLEN
              I won't. Not yet. Not as long as we both
              can stand it.

                              ARCHER
              This is not a life for you.

                              ELLEN
              It is. As long as it's part of yours.

                              ARCHER
              And the way I live...my life...how can it
              be part of yours?

She looks away. He reaches for her hands, holds them.

                              ELLEN
              Don't...don't be unhappy.

                              ARCHER
              You won't go back? You won't go back?

                              ELLEN
              I won't go back.

She lets go of his hands, turns and STANDS.

DISSOLVE TO ELLEN, moments later, leaving the room. ARCHER
remains seated.

DISSOLVE TO ARCHER, standing and following her out.

DISSOLVE TO THE EMPTY ROOM.

                                                    CUT TO

73 EXT. STREET/NEW YORK AUTUMN - DAY   73

    EXTREME LONG LENS SHOT of BROADWAY. SCREEN is FILLED with
    MEN, ARCHER among them, all coming toward us on their way
    to work, and all wearing the same derby.

    CUT TO sidewalk just outside Archer's law offices. The day
    is stifling, and a HOT WIND BLOWS from both rivers. MEN
    CLUTCH their derbies to their heads.

    ARCHER TURNS into the entrance of his office building as a
    MAN STEPS toward him. He is the SAME MAN Archer glimpsed
    outside the Parker House in Boston.

                        RIVIERE
                    (French accent)
              It's Mr. Archer, I think?

                        ARCHER
              Yes?

    In the BACKGROUND, as the men speak, several WOMEN walk by,
    holding their skirts down and their hats close.

                        RIVIERE
              My name is Riviere. We dined together
              in Paris last year.

                        ARCHER
              Oh yes. I'm sorry I didn't quite
              recall....

    And we should remember, as Archer does now, the face of the
    man with the fine mustache we first encountered during the
    Paris montage.

    People mill around them like rushing water as they stand
    talking.

                        RIVIERE
              Quite alright. I had the advantage.
              I saw you yesterday in Boston.

    Archer is taken aback by this.

                                                    CUT TO

74 INT. ARCHER'S OFFICE - DAY   74

    The window is closed because of the hot autumn wind, and
    heat has settled on the room like a curse. Occasional
    street NOISE, of pedestrians and carriage traffic, under-
    scores the conversation. Riviere seems slightly uncomfort-
    able, but handles himself impeccably. Both men perspire.

                                            (CONTINUED)

74 CONTINUED: 74

                              ARCHER

          I still do not understand why we're
          speaking.

                              RIVIERE

          I came here on Count Olenski's behalf
          because I believed...in all good
          faith...that it would be best for the
          Countess to return to him. I met her in
          Boston and told her all the Count had
          said. She did me the kindness of listening
          carefully. But she's changed, Monsieur.

                              ARCHER
                    (a tinge of jealous suspicion)
          You knew her before?

                              RIVIERE

          I used to see her in her husband's house.
          The Count would never have trusted my
          mission to a stranger.

                              ARCHER

          This change...

                              RIVIERE

          It may only have been my seeing her for
          the first time as she is. As an American.
          And if you're an American of her kind...of
          your kind...

CAMERA starts to move in on Archer.

                              RIVIERE

          ...things that are accepted in certain
          other societies, or at least put up with
          for the sake of...convenience...these
          things become intolerable. She made her
          marriage in good faith. It was a faith
          that the Count could not share, and
          could not understand. So her faith was
          shattered. And it was only coming back
          here...coming home...that restored it.
          Returning to Europe would mean a life of
          some comfort. And considerable sacrifice.
          And also, I would think, no hope.

Archer looks at his presidential calendar hanging on the
wall, then down at the papers scattered on his mahogany
desk.

(CONTINUED)

74 CONTINUED: (2)   74

He hears a SOUND—of a chair moving back, of Riviere getting
to his feet—and he looks up. Riviere is standing in front
of the desk.

                    RIVIERE
          I will fulfill my obligation to the Count
          and meet with the family. I will tell them
          what he wishes and suggests for the
          Countess. But I ask you, Monsieur, to use
          your own influence with them. I...I beg
          you...with all the force I'm capable
          of...not to let her go back.

Archer looks at him with astonishment. Riviere's eyes fix
momentarily on Archer, then look around the room. Archer
extends his hand.

                    ARCHER
          Thank you.

                                              CUT TO

75 INT. DINING ROOM/MRS. ARCHER'S HOUSE EVENING   75

A traditional Thanksgiving affair attended by Janey and
Mrs. Archer, Newland and May, Mrs. Welland and Sillerton
Jackson.

START ON MEDIUM CLOSE UP of turkey being carved on the
sideboard.

                    MRS. ARCHER (O.S.)
          Well, Boston is more conservative than New
          York. But I always think it's a safe rule
          for a lady to lay aside her French dresses
          for one season.

DISSOLVE TO MEDIUM CLOSE UP of sliced turkey being served.

                    MRS. ARCHER (O.S.)
          When Old Mrs. Baxter Pennilow died, they
          found her standing order—forty-eight Worth
          dresses—still wrapped in tissue paper.

DISSOLVE TO MEDIUM CLOSE UP of cranberry sauce in a crystal
serving dish.

                    MRS. ARCHER (O.S.)
          When her daughters left off their mourning
          they wore the first lot to the Symphony
          without looking in advance of the fashion.

                                              (CONTINUED)

75 CONTINUED: 75

DISSOLVE TO CAMERA TRACKING DOWN TABLE beside a SERVANT.
MRS. ARCHER continues talking as CAMERA moves away.

                    NARRATOR (V.O.)
          He had written to her once in Washington.
          Just a few lines, asking when they were to
          meet again. And she wrote back: "Not yet."

CAMERA, MOVING SLIGHTLY CLOSER, STOPS on ARCHER'S distracted
face just on those last two words. He barely notices the
SERVANT offering cranberry sauce.

                    JANEY
          I think it was Julius Beaufort who started
          the new fashion by making his wife clap
          her new clothes on her back as soon as
          they arrived. I must say, it takes all
          Regina's distinction not to look like...

                    JACKSON
               (helpfully)
          Her rivals?

                    JANEY
          ...like that Annie Ring.

                    MRS. ARCHER
          Careful, dear.

                    JANEY
          Well, everybody knows.

                    JACKSON
          Indeed. Beaufort always put his business
          around. And now that his business is gone
          there are bound to be disclosures.

                    MAY
          Gone? Is it that bad?

                    JACKSON
          As bad as anything I've ever heard of.
          Most everybody we know will be hit, one
          way or another.

CAMERA DOLLIES IN on JACKSON, ending in a MEDIUM CLOSE UP
as he speaks the last words.

                                              CUT TO

76 INT. LIBRARY/ARCHER HOUSE - NIGHT   76

Archer and Jackson stand in front of a painting in the
Gothic library. Archer helps Jackson light a cigar.

                    JACKSON
            (walking away to sit down)
        Very difficult for Regina, of course. And
        it's a pity...it's certainly a pity...that
        Countess Olenska refused her husband's
        offer.

                    ARCHER
        Why, for God's sake?

                    JACKSON
        Well...to put it on the lowest ground....
        what's she going to live on now?

                    ARCHER
        Now...?

ARCHER moves to sit down next to JACKSON.

                    JACKSON
        Well, I mean now that Beaufort...

                    ARCHER
        What the hell does that mean, sir?

                    JACKSON
            (continuing tranquilly)
        Most of her money's invested with
        Beaufort, and the allowance she's been
        getting from the family is so cut back...

                    ARCHER
She has something, I'm sure.

                    JACKSON
        Oh I would think a little. Whatever
        remains after sustaining Medora. But I
        know the family paid close attention to
        Monsieur Riviere and considered the
        Count's offer very closely. Everyone hopes
        the Countess herself might simply see that
        living here, on such a small margin...

(CONTINUED)

76 CONTINUED: 76

                              ARCHER
          If everyone would rather she be Beaufort's
          mistress than some decent fellow's wife,
          you've all gone about it perfectly.

     ARCHER bangs his BRANDY SNIFTER on the table and remains
     standing. Jackson looks at him attentively.

                              ARCHER
          She won't go back.

                              JACKSON
          That's your opinion, eh? Well no doubt you
          know. I suppose she might still soften
          Catherine Mingott, who could give her
          any allowance she chooses. But the rest
          of the family has no particular interest
          in keeping Madame Olenska here. They'll
          simply let her find her own level.

     Archer sees: a cone of ASH dropping from Jackson's cigar
     into a brass tray at his elbow.

                              ARCHER
                           (pause)
          Shall we go up and join my mother?

                                                          CUT TO

76A INT. ARCHER HOUSE HALLWAY - NIGHT   76A

     As May and Archer arrive home from Thanksgiving. Servants
     take their coats.
                                                          CUT TO

77 INT. ARCHER HOUSE - NIGHT   77

     Archer and May climb the staircase to the second floor of
     their house. The LAMP May holds throws deep long SHADOWS on
     the wall.

                              ARCHER
          The lamp is smoking again. The servants
          should see to it.

                              MAY
          I'm sorry.

     He stops at the door of his study. She stops and bends over
     to lower the wick. The light shines on her shoulders and
     the curve of her face.

                                                    (CONTINUED)

> ARCHER
>
> I may have to go to Washington for a few
> days.

> MAY
>
> When?

> ARCHER
>
> Tomorrow. I'm sorry, I should have said
> something before.

> MAY
>
> On business?

> ARCHER
>
> On business, of course. There's a patent
> case coming up before the Supreme Court. I
> just got the papers from Letterblair. It
> seems...

> MAY
>
> Never mind. I'm sure it's too complicated.
> I have enough trouble managing this lamp.

He helps her with the wick.

> MAY
>
> But the change will do you good.

The flame is stronger now.

> MAY
>
> And you must be sure to go and see Ellen.

He looks at her in the newly bright lamp light. Does she
know? He thinks she might.

                                                              CUT TO

78 INT. ARCHER HOUSE NIGHT   78

CAMERA close on a note being carried quickly on a silver
tray through the hall.

WIDER to show: a MAID, carrying the note to Archer and May.

> ARCHER MAID
>
> Excuse me, ma'am. But this came while you
> were out.

                                                         (CONTINUED)

May reaches for the note.

> ARCHER
> (indicating lamp)
> Do something about this, will you, Agnes?

He indicates the lamp, which still smokes slightly. The
maid nods, gives him her old lamp and takes the faulty one
away.

May looks up from the note.

> MAY
> Granny's had a stroke.

CUT TO

79 INT. BEDROOM, HALL, AND DRAWING ROOM/MINGOTT HOUSE - MORNING 79

Start on low angle of servants' FEET, walking slowly and
with difficulty...as if supporting some great weight. Mrs.
Mingott's elegantly slippered feet occupy the center of the
frame.

> MRS. MINGOTT
> A stroke! I told them all it was just an
> excess of Thanksgiving.

CAMERA PULLS OUT and TILTS UP from low angle to reveal MRS.
MINGOTT being carried by several SERVANTS in a heavy CHAIR
out of her bedroom as if she were some potentate from the
subcontinent. They move through the hall and into the drawing room. Aside from breathing a bit more heavily, the old
woman seems little the worse for wear, although her speech
is a trifle slurred. May and Archer walk beside her.

> MRS. MINGOTT
> Dr. Bencomb acted most concerned and
> insisted on notifying everyone as if it
> were the reading of my last testament. But
> I won't be treated like a corpse when I'm
> hardly an invalid.

The SERVANTS are having some difficulty managing the chair
at the entrance to the drawing room. ARCHER STEPS IN to
help out and prevent Mrs. Mingott from tipping out onto the
floor.

> MRS. MINGOTT
> You're very dear to come. But perhaps you
> only wanted to see what I'd left you.

(CONTINUED)

79 CONTINUED: 79

                              MAY
              Granny, that's shocking!

ARCHER and the SERVANTS set MRS. MINGOTT down as CAMERA
MOVES in for EXTREME CLOSE UP. She is in the drawing room,
in her accustomed spot.

                         MRS. MINGOTT
              It was shock that did this to me. It's all
              due to Regina Beaufort. She came here last
              night, and she asked me...

As she talks, we SEE what Archer IMAGINES...
                                                        CUT TO
80 EXT. MINGOTT HOUSE - NIGHT   80

The door opens and CAMERA moves in on the face of Regina
Beaufort. She wears a thick veil, and looks, for a moment,
like a figure from a Gothic novel.

                         MRS. MINGOTT (V.O.)
              ...she had the effrontery to ask me...to
              back Julius. Not to desert him, she said.
              To stand behind our common lineage in the
              Townsend family.
                                                        CUT TO
81 INT. DRAWING ROOM/MINGOTT HOUSE - NIGHT   81

The regal Regina Beaufort, dressed in black as if for
mourning, speaking animatedly to an intractable Mrs.
Mingott.

                         MRS. MINGOTT (V.O.)
              I said to her, "Honor's always been honor,
              and honesty's always been honesty, in
              Manson Mingott's house, and will be 'till
              I'm carried out feet first." And then...if
              you can believe it...she said to me...

CAMERA close on the tearful face of Regina Beaufort.

                         MRS. MINGOTT (V.O.)
              ..."But my name, Auntie. My name's Regina
              Townsend." And I said, "Your name was
              Beaufort when he covered you with jewels,
              and it's got to stay Beaufort now that
              he's covered you with shame."
                                                        CUT TO

82 INT. DRAWING ROOM/MINGOTT HOUSE - DAY   82

Mrs. Mingott finishes her story.

                    MRS. MINGOTT

So I gave out. Simply gave out. Now family
will be arriving from all over expecting a
funeral and they'll have to be enter-
tained. I don't know how many notes
Bencomb sent out.

                    ARCHER

If there's any way we can help...

                    MRS. MINGOTT

Well my Ellen is coming. I expressly asked
for her. She arrives this afternoon on the
train. If you could fetch her...

                    ARCHER

Of course. If May will send the brougham,
I can take the ferry.

                    MAY

          (the slightest pause)
There, you see, Granny. Everyone will be
settled.

                                        CUT TO

83 INT./EXT. CARRIAGE - DAY   83

     CAMERA STARTS high overhead and MOVES IN as ARCHER and MAY
     leave Mrs. Mingott's house and enter their carriage.

                    MAY

I didn't want to worry Granny. But how can
you meet Ellen and bring her back here if
you have to go to Washington yourself this
afternoon.

                    ARCHER

I'm not going. The case is off. Postponed.
I heard from Letterblair this morning.

                    MAY

Postponed? How odd. Mama had a note from
him this morning as well. He was concerned
about Granny but he had to be away. He was
arguing a big patent case before the
Supreme Court. You said it was a patent
case, didn't you?

(CONTINUED

83 CONTINUED: 83

> ARCHER
>
> Well, that's it. The whole office can't
> go. Letterblair decided to go this morn-
> ing.

CAMERA now holds them both in VERY TIGHT TWO SHOT.

> MAY
>
> Then it's not postponed?

The blood rises in Archer's face.

> ARCHER
>
> No. But my going is.

May looks away from him. CARRIAGE MOVES FORWARD and brings
ARCHER into a SINGLE TIGHT CLOSE UP before carrying him out
of frame.

>   CUT TO

84 EXT. TRAIN STATION - DAY   84

Close DISSOLVE onto a swarm of PASSENGERS disembarking in
EXTREME SLOW MOTION from a steam train that we can only see
in outline. The PASSENGERS walk toward the camera like
ghosts from the past.

> NARRATOR (V.O.)
>
> He knew it was two hours by ferry and
> carriage from the Pennsylvania terminus
> in Jersey City back to Mrs. Mingott's.

We see: Archer's face, searching the crowd for Ellen.

> NARRATOR (V.O.)
>
> All of two hours. And maybe a little more.

DISSOLVE to CLOSE UPS of PASSENGERS as they walk through
the steam, still in EXTREME SLOW MOTION and INTERCUT with
CLOSE UPS of FEET disembarking down the train's steel
steps.

DISSOLVE from a final face to ELLEN'S FACE, in the crowd.

As CAMERA MOVES BACK, and ARCHER is already at her side. He
MOTIONS for the PORTER carrying her bags to follow them,
then draws her arm through his.

> ARCHER
>
> You didn't expect me today?

>   (CONTINUED)

84 CONTINUED: 84

               ELLEN

     No.

               ARCHER

     It was Granny Mingott who sent me. She's
     much better. I nearly went to Washington
     to see you. We would have missed each
     other.

They are at the carriage. CAMERA PULLS BACK NOW to show
OTHER TRAVELERS all around them: the faces of the recently
wealthy, the poor and the newly emerging middle class. This
is the only time that we glimpse a suggestion of a world
outside the rigid borders of society. As all these TRAVEL-
ERS swarm around them, ARCHER helps ELLEN into the carriage.

                                                        CUT TO

85 INT. CARRIAGE - DAY   85

     DISSOLVE quickly into Ellen seated in the carriage, Archer
     sitting close beside her.

               ARCHER

     Did you know...I hardly remembered you.

               ELLEN

     Hardly remembered?

               ARCHER

     I mean...I mean it's always the same. Each
     time I see you. You happen to me all over
     again.

               ELLEN

     Oh yes. I know, I know. For me too.

She puts her hand in his. The carriage starts to move.

Quick series of close DISSOLVES: he bends over. He UNBUT-
TONS her tight brown glove. He KISSES the palm of her hand.
She turns her hand over and CARESSES his cheek.

                                                        CUT TO

86 INT. CARRIAGE - DUSK   86

     Later on in the journey to Mrs. Mingott's. Ellen and Archer
     sit very close in the cab. A WIND blows outside.

                                                        (CONTINUED)

> ARCHER
>
> Your husband's secretary came to see me.
> The day after we met in Boston.

She seems surprised.

> ARCHER
>
> You didn't know?

> ELLEN
>
> No. But he told me he had met you. In
> Paris, I think.

> ARCHER
>
> Ellen...I have to ask you. Just one thing.

> ELLEN
>
> Yes?

> ARCHER
>
> Was it Riviere who helped you get away
> after you left your husband?

> ELLEN
>
> Yes. I owe him a great debt.

> ARCHER
>   (quietly)
> I think you're the most honest woman I
> ever met.

> ELLEN
>   (slight smile)
> No. But probably one of the least fussy.

> ARCHER
>
> Ellen, we can't stay like this.It can't
> last.

> ELLEN
>
> What?

> ARCHER
>
> Our being together and not being together.
> It's impossible.

> ELLEN
>
> You shouldn't have come today.

(CONTINUED)

Suddenly she turns to him and flings her arms around him,
pressing him CLOSE, kissing him passionately. He returns
all her feeling.

The LIGHT from a gas lamp on the street flashes in through
the window and makes her draw away, suddenly silent and
motionless, to the corner of the carriage.

> ARCHER

Don't be afraid. Look, I'm not even trying
to touch your sleeve. Being like this
isn't what I want. I need you with me. I
can even just sit still, like this, and
look at you.

> ELLEN

I think we should look at reality, not
dreams.

> ARCHER
>
> (desperate)

I just want us to be together.

> ELLEN

I can't be your wife, Newland. Is it
your idea I should live with you as
your mistress?

> ARCHER

I want...somehow I want to get away with
you. Find a world where words like that
won't exist.

> ELLEN

Oh my dear...where is that country? Have
you ever been there? Is there anywhere we
can be happy behind the backs of people
who trust us?

> ARCHER

I'm beyond caring about that.

> ELLEN

No you're not! You've never been beyond
that. I have. I know what it looks like. A
lie in every silence. It's no place for
us.

(CONTINUED)

86 CONTINUED: (3)   86

He looks at her, dazed. Then he reaches for the small cab
bell that signals orders to the coachman.

The coach pulls up. Archer starts out.

>   ELLEN
>   Why are we stopping? This isn't Granny's.

>   ARCHER
>   No. I'll get out here.

He steps down to the street.

>   ARCHER
>   You were right. I shouldn't have come
>   today.

He closes the door.

                                              CUT TO

87 EXT. STREET - DUSK   87

Archer signals and the coach pulls away.

The wind blows stronger. Archer HOLDS his HAT and TOUCHES
his eyes. There are TEARS.

He turns and walks away down the street.

                                              CUT TO

88 INT. LIBRARY/ARCHER HOUSE - NIGHT   88

Start on CLOSE UP of Japanese print. CUT TO Archer, LOOKING
at the print in a beautiful leather-bound book, which is
now in lower left of frame.

May is embroidering a sofa cushion. Firelight casts a
strong glow in the room.

Archer looks up from his book, SEES: May's arms, as she
works the needle. The sleeves of her dress have slipped
back. Her sapphire betrothal ring shines on her left hand
above her wedding band.

May sees him looking at her, smiles.

>   MAY
>   What are you reading?

>   ARCHER
>   Oh, a history. About Japan.

                                          (CONTINUED)

88 CONTINUED: 88

                         MAY

          Why?

                         ARCHER

          I don't know. Because it's a different
          country.

                         MAY

          You used to read poetry. It was so nice
          when you read it to me.

He gets to his feet.

                         ARCHER

          I need some air.

He goes to the window, opens it, leans out into the cold.

                         MAY

          Newland! You'll catch your death.

                         ARCHER

          Catch my death. Of course.

He turns, shuts the window, looks at May, who has gone back
to her embroidery.

                         NARRATOR (V.O.)

          But then he realized, I am dead. I've been
          dead for months and months.

CAMERA moves closer on him, watching May.

                         NARRATOR (V.O.)

          Then it occurred to him that she might
          die. People did. Young people, healthy
          people, did. She might die, and set him
          free.

May sees him looking at her.

                         MAY

          Newland?

He walks to her and touches her head.

                         ARCHER

          Poor May.

                                              (CONTINUED)

88 CONTINUED: (2)   88

> MAY
>
> Poor? Why poor?

> ARCHER
>
> Because I'll never be able to open a
> window without worrying you.

> MAY
>
> I'll never worry if you're happy.

> ARCHER
>
> And I'll never be happy unless I can open
> the windows.

> MAY
>
> In this weather?

CUT TO

89 Ext. STREET/ELLEN'S HOUSE - NIGHT   89

Light SNOW. Ellen comes down the front steps of her house
toward a carriage that waits for her at the curb.

As she approaches the carriage door, Archer steps out of
the shadows.

> ARCHER
>
> I have to see you. I didn't know when you
> were leaving again.

> ELLEN
>
> I'm due at Regina Beaufort's. Granny lent
> me her carriage.

> ARCHER
>
> With all that's happened, you're still
> going to see Regina Beaufort?

> ELLEN
>
> I know. Granny says Julius Beaufort is a
> scoundrel. But so is my husband, and the
> family still wants me to go back to him.

Two FIGURES, illuminated by the glowing street lamps but
still a little indistinct in the blowing snow, are walking
down the street toward Ellen and Archer.

> ARCHER
>
> But you won't go back?

(CONTINUED)

                          ELLEN

          No. Granny's asked me to stay and help
          care for her. But I think it's me she
          means to help. She said I've lived too
          long locked up in a cage. She's even seen
          to my allowance.

The two figures draw nearer, then discretely cross to the
other side of the street. As they pass under the streetlight we recognize one of the two men: LARRY LEFFERTS.

Archer and Ellen see them and draw a little closer to the
sheltering shadow of the carriage.

                          ARCHER

          You won't need my help if you have
          Granny's.

                          ELLEN

          I will still need your help. If I stay, we
          will have to help each other.

                          ARCHER

          I have to see you. Somewhere we can be
          alone.

                          ELLEN
                    (smiles)
          In New York?

                          ARCHER

          Alone. Somewhere we can be alone. There's
          the art museum in the park. Half past two
          tomorrow. I'll be at the door.

She nods and takes his arm. He helps her quickly into the
carriage.

We SEE: her gloved HAND GLIDING off his.

                                                      CUT TO

90 INT. ART MUSEUM - DAY   90

An obscure gallery in the brand new Metropolitan Museum.

CAMERA starts close on ELLEN's EYES, behind the mesh of a
veil.

DISSOLVE TO a case full of beautiful pre-Roman antiquities
with REFLECTIONS of sarcophagi or larger sculpture in the
glass. The ancient objects are in the foreground; in the

                                                   (CONTINUED)

background, clearly visible, are the faces of ARCHER and
ELLEN, studying the objects.

DISSOLVE TO a small, delicate piece of sculpture with a
legend underneath on a handwritten museum card: "Use
Unknown."

DISSOLVE to Archer and Ellen, sitting on a divan near a
heating system in the center of the room. Through the far
door is a diminishing perspective of other galleries.

Even though they are alone in the room, they both speak
softly. Their WHISPERS are sibilant in these marble walls.

                    ARCHER

          You came to New York because you were
          afraid.

                    ELLEN

          Afraid?

                    ARCHER

          Of my coming to Washington.

                    ELLEN

          I promised Granny to stay in her house
          because I thought I would be safer.

                    ARCHER

          Safer from me?

She bends her head.

                    ARCHER

          Safer from loving me?

EXTREME CLOSE-UP. What Archer sees: a tear, hanging in the
mesh of her veil.

                    ELLEN
                  (pause)
          Shall I come to you once, and then go
          home?

He doesn't answer. She gets up and starts out. He CATCHES
HER by the arm.

                    ARCHER

          Come to me once, then.

                                              (CONTINUED)

90 CONTINUED: (2)   90

They look at each other almost like enemies.

                         ARCHER
                       (pressing)
                 When? Tomorrow?

                         ELLEN
                       (hesitating)
                 The day after.

She moves away down the long gallery. He follows her.

                         ELLEN
                 No. Don't come any farther than this.

She hurries to the gallery door, turns, then leaves.

DISSOLVE from her, small in the distance, framed in the
gallery door, to...
                                                    CUT TO

91 INT. LIBRARY/ARCHER HOUSE - NIGHT   91

Archer is at his desk. An envelope addressed to Ellen is
near him; his pen is poised over a piece of vellum on which
he is writing an address for their rendezvous. A KEY, to go
with the address, is ready to be sealed in the envelope as
he looks up, slightly startled...

...as May enters, a little agitated.

                         MAY
                 I'm sorry I'm late. You weren't worried,
                 were you?

He SWEEPS the key, envelope and address into his desk drawer
before she is near enough to notice.

                         ARCHER
                 Is it late?

She removes her velvet hat as she speaks, drawing the long
hatpins from her glistening hair.

                         MAY
                 Past seven. I stayed at Granny's because
                 Cousin Ellen came in.

Archer reacts to the mention of Ellen's name. May doesn't
seem to notice.
                                              (CONTINUED)

91 CONTINUED: 91

>   MAY
>
>   We had a wonderful talk. She was so dear.
>   Just like the old Ellen. And Granny's so
>   charmed by her.

He listens to this, still beguiled by her apparent kind-
ness.

>   MAY
>
>   You do see, though, why sometimes the
>   family has been annoyed? Going to see
>   Regina Beaufort in Granny's carriage...

Now he gets up, annoyed at the same old prattle.

>   ARCHER
>
>   Aren't we dining out?

He starts past her, and she moves forward, almost impul-
sively. She throws her arms around him and presses her
cheek to his.

>   MAY
>
>   You haven't kissed me today.

She is trembling.

                                                         CUT TO

92 INT. THEATER - NIGHT   92

CAMERA looks down on May from above. She is sitting serenely
in a theater box. She wears a beautiful dress of blue-white
satin and old lace.

CAMERA moves in slowly to her as we hear...

>   NARRATOR (V.O.)
>
>   It was the custom, in old New York, for
>   brides to appear in their wedding dress
>   during the first year or two of marriage.
>   But May, since returning from Europe,
>   had not worn her bridal satin until this
>   evening.

On those last words, we quickly see...

CAMERA close on a bright bunch of DAISIES; petals being
sprinkled on the ground.

MUSIC up: it is the yearly performance of Faust. A woman
starts to sing an aria.

                                                    (CONTINUED)

92 CONTINUED: 92

In a reprise of the opening scene, we DISSOLVE to the face
of Newland Archer, who is surveying the audience from the
back of the club box. CAMERA PANS (his POV) as he looks
across the row of boxes, sees: MAY, in her wedding dress.

Then he looks over to the Mingott box, where he first saw
Ellen Olenska. It is empty.

                                                        CUT TO

93 INT. THEATER - NIGHT   93

As in the opening scene: Archer's POV as he walks quickly
down the theater corridor, past its red velvet walls.

                                                        CUT TO

94 INT. THEATER - NIGHT   94

CAMERA on Archer, tight, as he enters box and leans over to
May.

                          ARCHER
            My head's bursting. Don't tell anyone,
            but please come home with me.

May looks at him, then whispers to her mother. Mrs. Welland
whispers an excuse to her companion, Mrs. van der Luyden,
as May rises and leaves with her husband.

As she goes, she puts her hand on his.

                                                        CUT TO

95 INT. LIBRARY/ARCHER HOUSE - NIGHT   95

Starting with CAMERA close on Archer's hand as he opens a
silver box and takes out a cigarette.

CAMERA pans with cigarette, as we hear...

                          MAY
            Shouldn't you rest?

Archer walks to the fireplace, May near him.

                          ARCHER
            My head's not as bad as that. And there's
            something important I have to tell you
            right away.

May sits down in an armchair, looking at him expectantly.
Archer's library is newly decorated with dark embossed
paper, Eastlake bookcases and writing table.

                                                        (CONTINUED)

> ARCHER

May...There's something I've got to tell you....about myself....

May sits still. Her face is tranquil, but very pale.

> ARCHER

Madame Olenska...

> MAY
>
> (interrupting)

Oh, why should we talk about Ellen tonight?

> ARCHER

Because I should have spoken before.

> MAY

Is it really worthwhile, dear? I know I've been unfair to her at times. Perhaps we all have. You've understood her better than any of us, I suppose. But does it matter, now that it's all over?

> ARCHER

Over? How do you mean, over?

> MAY

Why, since she's going back to Europe so soon.

Archer's hand grips the corner of the mantelpiece.

> MAY

Granny approves and understands. She's disappointed, of course, but she's arranged to make Ellen financially inde-pendent of the Count. I thought you would have heard today at your offices.

He stares, not really seeing her. She lowers her eyes.

Silence.

A lump of coal falls forward in the grate. May gets up to push it back and Archer turns to face her.

> ARCHER

It's impossible.

(CONTINUED)

                    MAY

Impossible? Certainly she could have
stayed here, with Granny's extra money.
But I guess she's given us up after all.

                  ARCHER

How do you know that?

                    MAY

From Ellen. I told you I saw her at
Granny's yesterday.

                  ARCHER

And she told you yesterday?

                    MAY

No. She sent me a note this afternoon.
Do you want to see it?

May moves to the desk and pulls the note from a small pile
of mail on the desk.

                    MAY

I thought you knew.

She holds out a note. He moves to her and takes it.

As CAMERA MOVES IN very close on Archer now, the LIGHTING
in the room seems to FADE. There are SHADOWS like slanted
bands across his face.

                 ELLEN (V.O.)

"May dear, I have at last made Granny
understand that my visit to her could be
no more than a visit, and she has been as
kind and generous as ever. She sees now
that if I return to Europe I must live by
myself. I am hurrying back to Washington
to pack up, and I sail next week. You must
be very good to Granny when I'm gone...as
good as you've always been to me."

We see Archer's head now in CLOSE UP. His EYES, reading the
note, are ILLUMINATED by a single strip of LIGHT.

                 ELLEN (V.O.)

"If any of my friends wish to urge me to
change my mind, please tell them it would
be utterly useless."

                                        (CONTINUED)

95 CONTINUED: (3)   95

LIGHT in the room COMES UP as Archer looks away from the
note to May.

> ARCHER
>
> Why did she write this?

> MAY
>
> I suppose because we talked things over
> yesterday.

> ARCHER
>
> What things?

> MAY
>
> I told her I was afraid I hadn't been
> fair to her. I hadn't always understood
> how hard it must have been here.

Archer is struggling hard to keep himself together.

> MAY
>
> I knew you'd be the one friend she could
> always count on. And I wanted her to know
> that you and I were the same. In all our
> feelings.
>   (more slowly)
> She understood why I wanted to tell her
> this. I think she understands everything.

She takes one of his cold hands and presses it quickly to
her cheek.

> MAY
>
> My head aches, too. Good night, dear.

She turns and walks toward the door. Her wedding dress
makes a soft SOUND in the still room.

                                                    CUT TO

96 INT. DINING ROOM/ARCHER HOUSE - NIGHT   96

CAMERA moves down the long dining room table, seeing: open-
work silver baskets, containing Maillard bonbons, placed
between candelabra; a lavish centerpiece of Jacqueminot
roses and maidenhair; the finest china and silver; handwritten dinner menus edged in gold.

                                                    (CONTINUED)

96 CONTINUED: 96

NARRATOR (V.O.)

It was, as Mrs. Archer said to Mrs.
Welland, a great event for a young couple
to give their first dinner, and it was not
to be undertaken lightly. There was a
hired chef, two borrowed footmen, roses
from Henderson's, Roman punch and menus on
gilt-edged cards. It was considered a particular triumph that the van der Luydens,
at May's request, stayed in the city to be
present at her farewell dinner for the
Countess Olenska.

Big CLOSE-UP of Archer. He goes through the motions of eat-
ing, but he has the face of a man in suspended animation.

CAMERA MOVES slowly out from him. First we see who's seated
on Archer's left: ELLEN, wearing several rows of amber
beads around her neck.

NARRATOR (V.O.)

Archer saw all the harmless-looking people
at the table as a band of quiet conspira-
tors, with himself, and Ellen, the center
of their conspiracy.

Gradually shot widens to include the room: there is a piano
in a corner with a large basket of flowers.

NARRATOR (V.O.)

He guessed himself to have been, for
months, the center of countless silently
observing eyes and patiently listening
ears. He understood that, somehow, the
separation between himself and the partner
of his guilt had been achieved. And he
knew that now the whole tribe had rallied
around his wife.

CAMERA (crane) ends on overhead shot of room: about twenty
GUESTS—including Mrs. Welland and Mrs. Archer, Janey and
the van der Luydens and the Lefferts and the Jacksons—are
enjoying the dinner and making easy conversation.

NARRATOR (V.O.)

He was a prisoner in the center of an
armed camp.

Now we see: CLOSE-UP of Archer's dazed and troubled face.
Table chatter continues. We hear, over...

(CONTINUED)

> JANEY
>
> Regina's not well at all, but that doesn't
> stop Beaufort from devoting as much time
> to Annie Ring...

As conversation drones on, CAMERA tilts down toward
Archer's coat pocket, and we DISSOLVE...

...through his coat...

...inside his pocket...

...to a sealed envelope, with his name and address on the
outside...

...through this envelope...

...to a SECOND ENVELOPE, the one which Archer addressed to
Ellen...

...through this envelope to the vellum, with their rendezvous address...

...and the key, lying beside the address in the folded
note.

Now CUT back to CLOSE-UP of Archer. PULL OUT to TWO SHOT
with Ellen sitting next to him. In an act of will, he turns
to her.

> ARCHER
>
> Was the trip from Washington very tiring?

> ELLEN
>
> The heat in the train was dreadful. But
> all travel has its hardships.

> ARCHER
>
> Whatever they may be, they're worth it.
> Just to get away.

She can't reply.

> ARCHER
>
> I mean to do a lot of traveling myself
> soon.

Ellen's face trembles. To rescue the moment, he leans
toward a man sitting across from him.

96 CONTINUED: (3)   9

                         ARCHER
          Philip, what about you? A little
          adventure? A long trip? Are you
          interested? Athens and Smyrna and
          maybe Constantinople. Then as far
          East as we can go.

                         PHILIP
          Possibly, possibly.

                   MRS. VAN DER LUYDEN
          But not Naples. Dr. Bencomb says there's
          a fever.

                         ARCHER
          There's India, too.

                         PHILIP
          You must have three weeks to do India
          properly.

                                                        CUT TO

97 INT. LIBRARY/ARCHER HOUSE - NIGHT   9'

     After dinner. The men are gathered in several groups, all
     smoking cigars. Archer still seems to be disengaged from
     everything happening around him, even though he manages to
     maintain appearances.

     CAMERA starts close on group of several men near Archer.

                         LEFFERTS
          Beaufort may not receive invitations
          anymore, but it's clear he still maintains
          a certain position.

                         PHILIP
          Horizontal, from all I've heard.

     CAMERA moves out to include others in group: Larry
     Lefferts, van der Luyden, Sillerton Jackson.

                         LEFFERTS
                      (indignant)
          If things go on like this, we'll be seeing
          our children fighting for invitations to
          swindlers' houses and marrying Beaufort's
          bastards.

                                              (CONTINUED)

97 CONTINUED: 97

                          JACKSON
         Has he got any?

Laughter from the group.

                          GUEST
         Careful, there, gentlemen. Draw it mild,
         draw it mild.

Archer manages a small smile, but is still distracted. He
starts to walk straight toward the CAMERA.

CAMERA pans with him as he goes. Van der Luyden comes to
his side (from left side of frame) and gently takes his
elbow. We see, in TWO-SHOT: van der Luyden, in profile, as
he speaks to Archer. Archer's back is turned.

                          VAN DER LUYDEN
         Have you ever noticed? It's the people who
         have the worst cooks who are always
         yelling about being poisoned when they
         dine out. Lefferts used to be a little
         more adept, I thought. But then, grace is
         not always required. As long as one knows
         the steps.

As van der Luyden speaks, the dialogue FADES and CAMERA
moves in on Archer, back still turned to us, lost in his
own thoughts. We end on tight CLOSE-UP of the back of
Archer's head. Behind him, the wall SHIFTS COLOR (to a deep
lavender or dark red) as we...

                                                    CUT TO

98 INT. HALLWAY/ARCHER HOUSE - NIGHT   98

CAMERA in tight CLOSE-UP of Archer's face. PULL BACK to
see: Archer, standing in the doorway of the drawing room.
Over his shoulder, we see other men coming down from the
library to join the ladies.

PAN from Archer slowly across room. We see MAY, sitting on
a gilt sofa next to Countess Olenska. MAY looks over, sees
Archer. Her eyes are shining as she gets up.

As soon as she's on her feet, Mrs. van der Luyden beckons
ELLEN to join her across the room.

Mrs. van der Luyden is standing next to a tall period POR-
TRAIT displayed on an easel. Having the painting situated
in the room this way makes the subject of the portrait, a
woman in formal dress, seem almost to be living, another
party guest. ELLEN comes slowly toward Mrs. van der Luyden,
and ANOTHER WOMAN joins them.

                                          (CONTINUED)

98 CONTINUED: 98

CAMERA pans with all this careful social choreography.
ARCHER watches the ritual as if it were an elaborate
rehearsal for a firing squad. We hear...

NARRATOR (V.O.)
The silent organization which held this
whole small world together was determined
to put itself on record. It had never for
a moment questioned the propriety of
Madame Olenska's conduct. It had never
questioned Archer's fidelity. And it
had never heard of, suspected, or even
conceived possible, anything at all to
the contrary.

CAMERA pans across the roomful of guests chatting with languid animation.

NARRATOR (V.O.)
From the seamless performance of this
ritual, Archer knew that New York believed
him to be Madame Olenska's lover.

CAMERA now on May.

NARRATOR (V.O.)
And he understood, for the first time,
that his wife shared the belief.

May looks at him and smiles.

CUT TO

99 INT. FRONT HALL/ARCHER HOUSE - NIGHT   99

CAMERA (Archer's POV) swoops down on Ellen's bare shoulders
in a great desperate rush.

Archer is helping her on with her cloak. Other GUESTS are
leaving. A sharp wind comes through the open door, making
the candlelight in the hallway flicker.

ARCHER
Shall I see you to your carriage?

She turns to him as Mrs. van der Luyden, swathed in sable,
steps forward.

MRS. VAN DER LUYDEN
(casual)
We are driving dear Ellen home.

(CONTINUED)

99 CONTINUED: 99

Ellen, grasping her fan of eagle feathers and holding her
cloak closed, offers her hand to Archer.

>   ELLEN

> Good-bye.

>   ARCHER

> Good-bye. But I'll see you soon in Paris.

>   ELLEN

> Oh...if you and May could come...

Mr. van der Luyden comes forward to offer his arm. She
takes it, and walks down the steps of the house.

Archer watches from the doorway. He sees:

Ellen, stepping into the carriage. For a moment, as she
gets herself settled, he can see her FACE in the dim
streetlight.

Then she sits back, and she is LOST in shadow.

                                              CUT TO

100 INT. UPPER HALLWAY/ARCHER HOUSE - NIGHT   100

May, holding a lamp, climbs the stairs of the now silent
house. Archer is a few steps behind her.

He stops, and goes toward the open door of the library.

May keeps going.

                                              CUT TO

101 INT. LIBRARY/ARCHER HOUSE - NIGHT   101

Archer looks lost in the room. May, pale but still full of
energy after the long night, now appears in the doorway.

>   MAY

> It did go off beautifully, didn't it?

>   ARCHER

> Oh. Yes.

>   MAY

> May I come in and talk it over?

>   ARCHER

> Of course. But you must be very sleepy.

                                         (CONTINUED)

101 CONTINUED: 101

                    MAY
          No. I'm not. I'd like to be with you a
          little.

                    ARCHER
          Fine.

They sit in separate chairs near the fire.

                    ARCHER
                (pause)
          Since you're not tired and want to talk,
          there's something I have to tell you. I
          tried the other night.

                    MAY
          Oh yes, dear. Something about yourself?

                    ARCHER
          About myself, yes. You say you're not
          tired. But I am. I'm tired of everything.
          I want to make a break...

                    MAY
          You mean give up the law?

                    ARCHER
          Well, maybe. To get away, at any rate.
          Right away. On a long trip. Go somewhere
          that's so far...

                    MAY
          How far?

                    ARCHER
          I don't know. I thought of India. Or
          Japan.

She stands up and walks toward him.

                    MAY
          As far as that? But I'm afraid you can't,
          dear...
                (unsteady voice)
          ...not unless you take me with you. That
          is, if the doctors will let me go...but
          I'm afraid they won't.

He stares at her, his eyes nearly wild.

(CONTINUED)

                         MAY

        I've been sure of something since this
        morning and I've been longing to tell
        you...

She sinks down in front of him, puts her face against his
knee.

                        ARCHER

        Oh.

He strokes her hair with his cold hand.

                         MAY

        You didn't guess?

                        ARCHER

        No. Of course, I mean, I hoped, but...

He looks away from her.

                        ARCHER
                      (quietly)
        Have you told anyone else?

                         MAY

        Only Mama, and your mother.
                      (a beat)
        And Ellen. You know I told you we'd
        had a long talk one afternoon...and
        how wonderful she was to me.

                        ARCHER

        Ah.

                         MAY

        Did you mind my telling her, Newland?

                        ARCHER

        Mind? Why should I? But that was two weeks
        ago, wasn't it? I thought you said you
        weren't sure till today.

                         MAY
                    (face flushed)
        No. I wasn't sure then. But I told her
        I was. And you see...

(CONTINUED)

She looks up at him, moving closer.

                              MAY
          I was right.

She is very close to him now, expecting to be kissed. Her
eyes are wet with VICTORY.

CAMERA close on Newland. He's speechless. He averts his
eyes.

CAMERA follows his desperate gaze around the room. It
starts to PAN slowly. After several moments we hear...

                    NARRATOR (V.O.)
          It was the room in which most of the real
          things of his life had happened.

CAMERA continues to PAN slowly around the room, from left
to right.

                    NARRATOR (V.O.)
          Their eldest boy, Theodore, too delicate
          to be taken to church in midwinter, had
          been christened there.

DISSOLVE to another PAN, moving in the same direction: a
baby being christened by an Episcopal bishop. May, Archer
and the rest of the family standing by, proud and pleased.

DISSOLVE to PAN continuing slowly across room. We begin to
notice gradual changes: in the furniture; in the furnishings; in the lighting.

                    NARRATOR (V.O.)
          It was here that Ted took his first steps.
          And it was here that Archer and his wife
          always discussed the future of all their
          children. Bill's interest in archeology.
          Mary's passion for sport and philanthropy.
          Ted's inclinations toward "art" that led
          to a job with an architect, as well as
          some considerable redecoration.

CAMERA pans slowly past a Chippendale cabinet and some
English mezzotints.

DISSOLVE to PAN in same direction, tighter than the one
before: of Mary, a stalwart young girl, being embraced by a
happy, older May.

                                                    (CONTINUED)

> NARRATOR (V.O.)
>
> It was in this room that Mary had
> announced her engagement to the dullest
> and most reliable of Larry Lefferts'
> many sons. And it was in this room, too,
> that her father had kissed her through
> her wedding veil before they motored to
> Grace Church.

DISSOLVE to PAN in same direction, very tight: of Archer
kissing his daughter through the veil.

DISSOLVE to continuing PAN of the library.

> NARRATOR (V.O.)
>
> He was a dutiful, loving father, and a
> faithful husband. When May died of
> infectious pneumonia after nursing Bill
> safely through, he had honestly mourned
> her. The world of her youth had fallen
> into pieces and rebuilt itself without
> her ever noticing.

CAMERA has completed pan of room, and now moves slowly in
on a silver-framed picture of the young May, dressed in her
Newport archery costume.

> NARRATOR (V.O.)
>
> This hard bright blindness, her incapacity
> to recognize change, made her children
> conceal their views from her, just as
> Archer concealed his. She died thinking
> the world a good place, full of loving and
> harmonious households like her own.

CAMERA is close on the picture, which rests on Archer's
Eastlake writing-table. Near it: a shaded electric lamp.
And the marble model of May's folded hands that was done in
Paris during their honeymoon.

> NARRATOR (V.O.)
>
> Newland Archer, in his fifty-seventh year,
> mourned his past and honored it.

We hear, for the first time: a SOUND that is both startling
and familiar...the RINGING of a telephone.

CAMERA PANS to phone, and to Archer's hand picking up the
receiver.

CAMERA follows the phone and reveals his face: at 57, he
shows the evidence of a full life behind him.

(CONTINUED)

                    ARCHER
Yes? Hello?

                    OPERATOR (V.O.)
Chicago wants you.

                    TED (V.O..)
Dad?

                    ARCHER
Ted?

                    TED (V.O.)
I'm just about finished out here, but my
client wants me to look at some gardens
before I start designing.

                    ARCHER
Fine. Where?

                    TED (V.O.)
Europe. I'll have to sail next Wednesday,
on the *Mauretania*.

                    ARCHER
And miss the wedding?

                    TED (V.O.)
Annie will wait for me. I'll be back on
the first and our wedding's not 'till the
fifth.

CAMERA starts to PAN around the room again. We hear the
rest of this conversation while seeing the other side of
the changed room.

                    ARCHER
                 (affectionate)
I'm surprised you remember the date.

                    TED (V.O.)
Well, I was hoping you'd join me. I'll
need you to remind me of what's important.
What do you say? It will be our last
father and son trip.

                    ARCHER
I appreciate the invitation, but...

                                          (CONTINUED)

101 CONTINUED: (6)   101

> TED (V.O.)
> Wonderful. Can you call the Cunard office
> first thing tomorrow?

CAMERA has come to rest on the window. Through the softly
blowing curtains we see: a sunny street on a fine New York
spring day.

And we...

DISSOLVE TO

102 INT. BRISTOL HOTEL ROOM/PARIS - DAY   102

Another window. Now the city is Paris, the street outside
the Faubourg St. Honore. The spring day is equally fine.

CAMERA pans around room, left-to-right. The luxurious
furnishings make a distinct contrast to Archer's darker,
subtler library. END on Archer, sitting on a divan near
the window, looking out.

A hand comes in and touches his shoulder. He turns: it's
Ted. He has his mother's bearing. But he has Archer's eyes.

> TED
> I'm going out to Versailles with Tourneur.
> Will you join us?

> ARCHER
> I thought I'd go to the Louvre.

> TED
> I'll meet you there later, then. Countess
> Olenska is expecting us at half-past five.

> ARCHER
>   (stunned)
> What?

> TED
> Oh, didn't I tell you. Annie made me swear
> to do three things in Paris. Get her the
> score of the last Debussy songs. Go to the
> Grand Guignol. And see Madame Olenska. You
> know she was awfully good to Annie when
> Mr. Beaufort sent her over to the
> Sorbonne.

(CONTINUED)

102 CONTINUED: 102

CAMERA moves close on Archer as his son talks, until only
Archer is in the frame. We see, in his face, signs of memories flooding back.

                         TED
          Wasn't the Countess friendly with Mr.
          Beaufort's first wife or something? I
          think Mrs. Beaufort said that she was.
          In any case, I called the Countess this
          morning and introduced myself as her
          cousin and...

                         ARCHER
          You told her I was here?

                         TED
          Of course. Why not? She sounds lovely. Was
          she?

                         ARCHER
          Lovely? I don't know. She was different.

                                              CUT TO

103 INSERT   103

A series of paintings of the Italian Renaissance, DISSOLV-
ING quickly from one to another.

                    NARRATOR (V.O.)
          Whenever he thought of Ellen Olenska, it
          had been abstractly, serenely, like an
          imaginary loved one in a book or picture.
          She had become the complete vision of all
          that he had missed.

Last painting of the short series is a Titian of almost
palpable sensuality.

HOLD on this as we hear...

                    ARCHER (V.O.)
                      (whispering)
          But I'm only fifty-seven.

And we...

                                              DISSOLVE TO

104 INT. LOUVRE/PARIS - DAY   104

    Archer's face, melancholy and uncertain now, studying the
Titian.

    Dazzles of afternoon light flood the gallery. He turns and
walks away.

                                        CUT TO

105 EXT. TUILERIES/PARIS - AFTERNOON   105

    Ted and Archer, deep in conversation, walk through the
great gardens on their way to Madame Olenska's.

                  TED

           Did Mr. Beaufort really have such a bad
           time of it, when he wanted to remarry? No
           one wanted to give him an inch.

                ARCHER

           Perhaps because he had already taken so
           much.

                TED

           As if anyone remembers any more. Or cares.

                ARCHER

           Well, he and Annie Ring did have a lovely
           daughter. You're very lucky.

                TED

           We're very lucky, you mean.

                ARCHER

           Yes, that's what I mean.

                TED

           So considering how that all turned
           out...and considering all the time that's
           gone by...I don't see how you can resist.

                ARCHER

           Well, I did have some resistance at first
           to your marriage, I've told you that...

                TED

           No, I mean resist seeing the woman you
           almost threw everything over for. Only you
           didn't.

                                      (CONTINUED)

105 CONTINUED: 105

> ARCHER
> (cautious)
>
> I didn't.

> TED
>
> No. But mother said...

> ARCHER
>
> Your mother?

> TED
>
> Yes. The day before she died. She asked to
> see me alone, remember? She said she knew
> we were safe with you, and always would
> be. Because once, when she asked you to,
> you gave up the thing you wanted most.

Archer walks on in silence for a few moments.

> ARCHER
>
> She never asked me.

CUT TO

106 EXT. RUE DU BAC/PARIS - DAY   106

A quiet quarter off a busy boulevard. Archer stands in a
little square, looking up at a contemporary building with
balconies running up its cream-colored front.

CAMERA (Archer's POV) MOVES across the surface of the
building.

> NARRATOR (V.O.)
>
> After a little while he did not regret
> Ted's indiscretion. It seemed to take an
> iron band from his heart to know that,
> after all, someone had guessed and
> pitied...And that it should have been his
> wife moved him inexpressibly.

Ted crosses the square to his father.

> TED
>
> The porter says it's the fifth floor.

He casually slips his arm through his father's.

> TED
>
> It must be the one with the awnings.

(CONTINUED)

They both look toward an upper balcony, just above the
horse-chestnut trees in the square. The day is fading into
a soft sun-shot haze. The sun makes reflections on the window.

Ted turns to his father.

> TED
>
> It's nearly six.

Archer sees an empty bench under a tree.

> ARCHER
>
> I think I'll sit a moment.

> TED
>
> Do you mean you won't come?

Archer shrugs.

> TED
>
> You really won't come at all?

> ARCHER
>
> I don't know.

> TED
>
> She won't understand.

> ARCHER
>
> Go on, son. Maybe I'll follow you.

He walks toward the bench, Ted following him.

> TED
>
> But what will I tell her?

> ARCHER
> (as he sits)
>
> Don't you always have something to say?

> TED
>
> I'll tell her you're old-fashioned and you
> insist on walking up five flights instead
> of taking the elevator.

> ARCHER
> (pause)
>
> Just say I'm old-fashioned. That should be
> enough.

(CONTINUED)

106 CONTINUED: (2)   106

Ted gives his father a look of affectionate exasperation,
then crosses the square and goes into the building.

Archer sits on the bench, watching him go.

Then he LOOKS UP at the windows on the fifth floor.

The setting SUN makes dazzling REFLECTIONS on the glass.

A CURTAIN moves, briefly, then falls back into place.

The sun suddenly makes a bright FLARE on the pane, stinging
Archer's eyes. He moves his head slightly and we...

                                                    CUT TO

107 EXT. SUMMER HOUSE/NEWPORT - DUSK   107

Another sunset, almost thirty years before.

A SAILBOAT starts to sail between the shore and a LIGHT-
HOUSE.

ELLEN, in the summer house, watches it. Her back is to us.

The SAILBOAT glides between the shore and the LIGHTHOUSE.
The SUN dances on the water.

ELLEN stands in the last brilliant burst of the setting
sun. She starts to move.

She TURNS AROUND.

And looks full at us, CAMERA close.

And SHE SMILES.

                                                 DISSOLVE TO

108 EXT. RUE DU BAC/PARIS - DAY   108

DISSOLVE onto balcony window. A servant starts to roll up
the awning.

WIDE SHOT of Archer, still on the bench, watching the
awning being secured. The servant finishes, goes back
inside.

Archer remains on the bench, alone in the twilight.

                                                    FADE OUT

                          THE END

SOURCES

Edith Wharton herself appears never to have entered a movie theater.
—R.W.B. Lewis, *Edith Wharton: A Biography*

At some point soon after shooting, with the editing not half done, Marty and I had one of our frequent weekend dinners. Over the years, these casual occasions had taken on their own agenda: catch up and decompress; swap stories; plan projects and trade memories; worry about whether we should have dessert. As the years went on, we found ourselves reminiscing more and more, keeping the memories immediate and alive and making sure no dust settled over the common ground.

This dinner, this time, was a little different. We both made an effort not to mention, directly or by inference, all the *Age* work still at hand. We tried not to mention the movie at all, but of course we couldn't do it. The movie kept coming up. Never directly, though; not at first.

We never spoke of a single editing intricacy, or structural problem. Instead, as we usually do, we started to talk about movies, in a loose, freely-associative way, closing quickly onto specific titles, talking about scenes, shots, performances, quirks of story, bits of production arcana. Somewhere around the third or fourth title, Marty looked up from his plate of chow fun and hooked me with one of those half-amused, half-skeptical looks I'd come to know well. He was on to something, and was waiting for the me to catch up and catch on.

Seeking to avoid being cast as Watson to my friend's perpetual Holmes, I rattled on, praising *The Strange Affair of Uncle Harry,* a Robert Siodmak movie I'd just seen again after many years, until Marty said, "I didn't think we'd talk about *The Age of Innocence.*"

There was no getting around it, never mind getting away from it. Each of the movies we'd spoken of up till that point had some bearing on *The Age of Innocence:* as an inspiration, as a source of stylistic or spiritual nourishment, even as a temporary tool. We were used to striking sparks from unexpected places—Marty had solved a thorny blocking problem in *Age* while we watched Robert Hamer's *Pink*

127

String and Sealing Wax—but we had not realized, till that night at dinner, just how wide a net we had cast in our Wharton adaptation.

Since this present book is an album of how influences become a confluence, we thought it might be interesting to pass along a few of the movies that, by mutual reckoning, found their way, one way or another, into *The Age of Innocence*. For us, anyway, it seems like a good time to try. Midpoint in the journey to a fixed, finished film, we find ourselves in a small clearing, still deep in the woods, looking all around, getting oriented by trying to figure how we got here in the first place.

This is how, as best we can work it out. This isn't a true filmography; it's a trail of celluloid breadcrumbs. But lurking wicked wolves, please take note: we're not putting ourselves up for membership in this company. These are simply movies that we admire, like and, in some cases, love; movies that, we reckon, somehow shaped and intrigued us. They are all part of *The Age of Innocence,* ghosts in the halls of the rambling house we've tenanted for a while.

This list does not reflect anything formal or definitive, either. Once we decided to include it in this book at all—a decision reached after realizing that, despite whatever we say, any one of these movies could and might be used to give us a reproving rap on the knuckles—we wanted to find a format that was as informal as possible. So, with some alphabetical ordering, general tinkering and the addition of the first person for me and the conventional but convenient third-person for Marty, this is a rough retrospective of our dinner conversation that evening. The requests for more chow fun and abject inquiries about dessert have been omitted.

We covered 22 titles. We might have overlooked as many more, and may have continued, too, except that there was still a movie to see that night: *London Town,* sometimes known as *My Heart Goes Crazy,* directed by Wesley Ruggles in 1946. I hope that will find its way onto another list, another time, for another film. Maybe, too, that's why we keep watching movies. To keep making them. Or, as Marty says, "to be inspired to make them. Or to be inspired to *try* and make them. Because nothing's automatic anymore, and the trying's the hardest."

That's pretty much what we tell anyone who asks why we see so many movies. We just say we're working. We keep the fun part to ourselves.

Nobody's fooled.

BARRY LYNDON (1975). *Director-Writer:* Stanley Kubrick.

Candles. Color. Narration. The slow zooms in and out that keep the audience just where Kubrick wants them: on the outside, as if admiring a landscape. Or—on the zoom in—closer and closer to the hard heart of this bleakly comic, ironic rake's progress. The Calvary of a simple man undone by fate, his own impetuosity and a recognizably pragmatic set of values. Far from *Age* in theme, but not, perhaps, in tone:

the chill, bemused irony of the narration—the lavish but careful use of the novelist's language—turns the drama gradually from shrewd observation of 18th-century English mores into a complex, poignant portrait of vanity and ambition. We even wrote some wild lines for Michael Gough in *Age* that recounted an incident from *Barry Lyndon* about death at a gaming club. They made for slightly racier conversation than usual at a formal dinner in 1870s New York, but it was a fair way of saying thanks.

CARRIE (1952). *Director:* William Wyler. *Writers:* Ruth and Augustus Goetz.

Unslakable love for a star-crossed, contradictory woman that leads to eventual ruin. The great Olivier, in one of his greatest film performances, using an American accent taught him by Spencer Tracy, is the increasingly unhinged lover; Jennifer Jones is his once-gained, then impossible object of desire. Another adaptation of a classic novel, Theodore Dreiser's *Sister Carrie*, this film was so strong and—we gather—so virulently downbeat in its original form that it was shelved for a year after its completion, then released in a truncated version that—according to Olivier—was also softened. What remains, however, is still extraordinary: Wyler's great contrast of spaciousness and claustrophobia, his formalism underscoring and holding in check—but just barely—the fatalistic fervor of the story. Would this be what might happen, eventually, to Archer and Ellen if they broke convention, betrayed what they loved and believed of each other, and went away together? We talked over this possibility—and a few others—but dared draw no conclusions. The contours of Wharton's plot have their own rigorous resolution.

DETOUR (1945). *Director:* Edgar G. Ulmer. *Writer:* Martin Goldsmith.

The kind of movie, resurrected and championed in the late '50s by the young cinema fiends of *Cahiers du Cinema*, that was used as a cudgel by skeptical American academics and hidebound reviewers to illustrate the folly of the auteurists. *Detour*, along with most other *Cahiers* favorites, has endured, while the denunciations, if remembered at all, seem simply shortsighted and blind-sided. An image from *Detour* occurred to Marty while writing a scene of Archer receiving a note that would effect him deeply, and turn the plot sharply. Marty flashed on the existential schmo hero of *Detour* ruing his fate while the screen grew dark around him, until only his eyes were vivid in a single band of light. The light looked like something filtering through the small rectangular window of a cell door in the solitary block. It was a bravura stylistic coup, but *Detour* has, on reflection, a bit more than a trick of the light in common with *Age*. Its grisly noir theatrics and all the vacuum-packed inventiveness of Ulmer's direction were at the service of a story, like *Age*, of two women and a man entangled in the unforgiving geometry of their own ardor. *Age*, on its surface, might have more elegance, but we'd count ourselves lucky to cut into some portion of *Detour's* corrosive intensity.

EXPERIMENT PERILOUS (1944). *Director:* Jacques Tourneur. *Writer:* Warren Duff.

A romantic thriller, set in the late Edwardian era in New York, with suggestions—like *Gaslight*—of dark doings in a marriage and dank obsessions lurking in the enfolding recesses of a great New York house. Tourneur was a master of unforced atmosphere: the menace here is almost palpable, but it never becomes too pronounced, even when the mystery is resolved in a way that's less imaginative than its meticulous creation. More shafts of light furnishing Marty with ideas: we hit the VCR to look over Tourneur's craftsmanship on several occasions, paying particular attention to the ways in which he used setting to reinforce atmosphere, not just to establish it. There was something almost—literally—dreamy in Tourneur's best movies, whether he was working in the realm of fantasy (*Cat People*), noir (*Out of the Past*) or horror (*Curse of the Demon*), but, if these played like dreams, they never seemed distanced, over-rarified by style. Their true mystery was in their simplicity.

FAR FROM THE MADDING CROWD (1967). *Director:* John Schlesinger.
Writer: Frederic Raphael.

Another classically inspired love story, from another classic (Thomas Hardy) source, made with grace and care, with attention not only to period but also to the imperatives of emotion that lead four brilliantly wrought and acted characters (Julie Christie, Alan Bates, Peter Finch, Terence Stamp) through a maze of intersecting destinies. Struggles against an enclosed society's expectations, battles against predestination that leave no victors on any side: the heart does not always find its way. The movie seemed—and still does—both of its period and very much of our time, even though its themes of love, expectation, and obligation are thought to be old-fashioned. When they are managed as well as they are here, however, we were relieved to realize that "old-fashioned" may merely mean "overlooked," and ready for rediscovery.

THE HEIRESS (1949). *Director:* William Wyler. *Writers:* Ruth and Augustus Goetz.

Henry James's *Washington Square*, evolved into a hard-grained story of romance and repression in 19th-century New York by the same team that would go on to *Carrie*. Precision balance of tension is maintained as a courtship is played out as a possible con game, and the influence of Europe compromises—perhaps corrupts—the paralyzed rectitude of American society. Wyler shoots drawing rooms, ballrooms and dining rooms as if they were antechambers of the soul, each filled with deep shadow and stalks of light, each holding some possible secret about a mystery that can never be solved. The implosive devastation of this movie's final scene—Olivia de Havilland ascending the steps of her house, lamp in hand, her face like a Mayan mask, leaving Montgomery Clift outside, pounding at the door, shut out forever—was a touchstone for our adaptation of *The Age of Innocence*. *The Heiress* is devastating and memorable in a far deeper way than Wyler's more warmly remembered *Wuthering Heights* because it is less sentimental. A woman is desolated, a man destroyed: all according to the murderous clockwork precision of societal order and social expectation.

THE INNOCENT (1977), THE LEOPARD (1963) and SENSO (1954). *Director:* Luchino Visconti. *Writers of* The Innocent: Suso Cecchi D'Amico, Enrico Medioli, Luchino Visconti. *Writers of* The Leopard: Luchino Visconti, Suso Cecchi D'Amico, Pasquale Festa Campanile, Enrico Medioli, Massimo Franciosa. *Writers of* Senso: Suso Cecchi D'Amico, Luchino Visconti, Giorgio Prosperi, Carlo Alianello, Giorgio Bassani, Tennessee Williams, Paul Bowles.

Visconti's supreme trilogy of political change and romantic dissolution in the 19th century. Some movies are inspiring; others are daunting. For us, these were both. When I passed the Wharton novel to Marty, I suggested that in milieu, it might remind him a little of these great films. *The Leopard,* especially, was a movie Marty had seen often over the years, almost as if the film itself were an act of sensual mesmerism. These Visconti films are all social pageants, on a vast scale that we could never hope to equal with *The Age of Innocence.* It would, indeed, have been inappropriate to try, just as it would have been an act of overweening hubris to set out to best, beat, even duplicate them. But *The Leopard* exerted an unremitting fascination. We knew that the ballrooms of aristocratic Sicily were a good deal different from the ballrooms of old New York, and if by some chance a Sicilian ballroom had found its way to this innocent age, it would have looked as seemly as a big top tent on a Newport lawn. Still, we couldn't forget the lush last sequence of *The Leopard,* any more than we'd want to extinguish a cherished recurring dream. Visconti remained crucial to us, not for scale or aspiration, but for spirit. He had found a way to work with period material—"classical era" material—that had stylistic breadth and psychological panache. There was nothing safe, small or simply pretty about these films. They had true contemporary pitch as well as an evocative epochal sense, great detail of mise-en-scène to match an unwavering sense of emotional grandeur that no one has ever approached again.

THE INNOCENTS (1961). *Director:* Jack Clayton. *Writers:* William Archibald, Truman Capote, John Mortimer.

Henry James again, this time a wonderful adaptation of *The Turn of the Screw* in which lurking late Victorian repression is embodied—or, rather, disembodied—in the specters that haunt a governess at a remote stately home. Few movies can match this one for sheer draughty terror and clinging menace. Few catch what we took to be the undertone of the time so tellingly. We had no ghosts, of course; but what the apparitions of the dead represent in *The Innocents* seemed a good point on which to sight our compass for *Age.* They are shades that spring from a stifled psyche, the issue of thoughts unspoken, feelings unexpressed and dreams that die in shame with the daylight. They were, for us, an expression of much that was deeply, secretly felt but never spoken in *Age*. And the house in *The Innocents*, with its endless hallways all leading deeper into darkness, was a full character, just as it was in Robert Wise's similar and also superb *The Haunting*. We hoped, in the same way, that each room in *The Age of Innocence* would be some refraction of the people living in it.

JULES AND JIM (1961) and TWO ENGLISH GIRLS (1972). *Director:* François Truffaut. *Writers:* François Truffaut, Jean Gruault.

Texts for style: the flutterpunch editing; the roving, restless camera, moving, panning, slowly zooming in practically every scene, never still; the narration, which broke rules by recounting how characters felt, and even, on occasion, describing what they were doing while they did it; the reliance on letters and notes and diaries, and the way they were presented. These films were more than an inspiration. We thought of them personally, intimately, as a kind of legacy. There was more for us within them than just style, however. *Jules and Jim*, especially, was liberating. We both saw it, separately but almost simultaneously, when it was first released in America. We were at an age that was not simply impressionable. We were frantic for exaltation, looking for a reflection of the fire we felt for filmmaking up on the screen. We found it in *Jules and Jim*. The movie reveled in cinema: it conveyed a giddy, unfettered joy in the process of filmmaking, as well as in all its possibilities. Those possibilities seemed, with Truffaut's eye, to be exactly what we felt, wanted and needed them to be: limitless. It was only later, after uncounted viewings, that we began to work into the depths of these two movies: the elegiac eroticism, the tremendous psychological tension, the tidal pull toward destruction from which the characters can't escape. As a small way of acknowledging debt and returning thanks, the name of the author of the two novels on which these films were based got tucked into *The Age of Innocence*. Truffaut— whose own name became too celebrated for easy inclusion—remains in *Age,* we hope, as a continual shaping presence, a guiding grace.

LETTER FROM AN UNKNOWN WOMAN (1948) and LOLA MONTES (1955). *Director:* Max Ophuls. *Writer of* Letter: Howard Koch. *Writers of* Lola Montes: Max Ophuls, Annette Wademant, Franz Geiger.

Ophuls was the cinema's foremost romantic. Perhaps its utmost. There were many others—Frank Borzage comes first to mind—but none cut sentiment with a saving shot of cynicism like Ophuls. These two movies, his best known, combine worldliness and fabulism with a kind of reflexive melancholy: the characters here are creatures of fate whose fates—in both cases—rush them past folly toward doom. And, of course, there are those camera moves. Dazzling tracking shots, splendiferous sweeps around the set. All the action seems orchestrated to a single heartbeat. What wonders would Ophuls have accomplished in these days of the Steadicam? His films, however bittersweet the story told, were all fashioned with a stylistic ebullience that made even the most somber of them shine with the joy of craft and the confidence of a storyteller giddy with his own skill.

MADAME BOVARY (1949). *Director:* Vincente Minnelli. *Writer:* Robert Ardrey.
Certainly, on the surface, this must have seemed a classic Hollywood mismatch: one of the greatest of all musical directors, adapting one of the most scrupulously unadorned of novels, a certifiable masterpiece of supple observation and social portraiture. But Minnelli knew himself better than most. Either that, or he discovered another dimension here, because his film—even with an odd framing device of Flaubert, in the dock, defending his novel against charges of obscenity—captures all the longing and desperation and wrongheaded, hopeless romanticism of Bovary, the willfulness that is winning and punishing at once. Minnelli's direction surprises with its uninsistent audacity. The film has a great set-piece: a dance that becomes rhythmic, then unrelenting, then vertiginous, till the ballroom windows have to be broken to give the women air. Minnelli fashions this into the perfect metaphor for Bovary's shut-in, stifled soul. The dance sequence is not aimlessly spectacular, but an extension of all the turmoil inside its main character. And Ellen Olenska must surely have read Flaubert.

MADELEINE (1949). *Director:* David Lean. *Writers:* Nicholas Phipps, Stanley Haynes.
Maybe we're just being contrary. David Lean poor-mouthed this movie something awful, treating it as an unrelieved embarrassment. Certainly it's an anomaly in a career that seemed to treat each fresh venture as some new, splendid exploration, as if Lean were last in the line of great 19th century adventurers, bushwhacking with crew and camera instead of rifle and porters. *Madeleine* was decidedly a side trip, not a safari, a side-show in a life full of pageant. But, like a carny on the far side of a cathedral, it exerts its own peculiar, compulsive, and slightly naughty fascination. The movie is full of penumbra and nightshade, an appropriate combination for a high melodrama involving passion and poison in the last great days of the Empire. Lean's bleak, frosty fascination with murder as fit retribution as well as orgasmic release gives the film a nippy and welcomely disreputable undercurrent. Ann Todd's blank blonde stare lingers in close-up like a Victorian cameo hand-painted by Whistler and sculpted by Tussaud's.

THE MAGNIFICENT AMBERSONS (1942). *Director-Writer:* Orson Welles.
A mutilated masterpiece—the *Greed* of the sound era—that, even in its tattered

state, holds a high ground that few other movies can begin to scale. Orson Welles's voice over a black screen—"The magnificence of the Ambersons began…"—echoes in the memory as (and we're willing to argue about this) the most seductive spoken invitation to the past in all movie history. *Ambersons* has been a particular obsession since I first saw it, on an old RCA television, on WOR New York's Channel 9, on a program called "Million Dollar Movie." For any movie-smitten kid in New York, "Million Dollar Movie" was a living-room Cinémathèque. It showed the RKO library once a night, twice on weekends: seven showings in all. Seven chances to see *King Kong* and *Bringing Up Baby* and *Gunga Din*. Seven chances, every one of them taken, to see *Citizen Kane*. And *Ambersons*. I was enthralled at the narrative sweep and stylistic virtuosity, the sheer voluptuous beauty of the film. I'd already read in the one book of film history in my Bronx library that the movie had been taken away from Welles, re-edited by the studio and severely compromised. I could tell *Kane* was a better movie, certainly more fully rounded and realized. I also knew, but could not work out why, I was more moved by *Ambersons* even than *Kane*. Marty shared much of my fascination, but not my full feeling. He admitted, at first, to being disappointed and confused by *Ambersons* after luxuriating in the finished pleasures of *Kane*. He was always troubled by the narrative and emotional gaps in *Ambersons*, its truncated rhythms and abrupt shifts of characterization. He could see its promise and potential, but the film—as well as its characters and milieu—remained a little alien to him. I recognized all these flaws in *Ambersons*, but loved the movie not only despite them, but, in another way, because of them: I could fill in the gaps myself, redirect the movie in my own imagination toward the perfection I was certain that Welles, left free, would have achieved. I hectored Marty constantly about this, and, after a while, may have succeeded in getting him to see the movie a little bit my way. Our discovery of the Criterion laser disc edition of *Ambersons*, which contained a script, stills and descriptions of deleted scenes, as well as a second-channel audio narration that explained what was missing and where it went, both crimped our imagination and confirmed the feeling that *Ambersons*, after *Kane*, would have been the greatest one-two punch in movie history, a sure knockout. And, as it always had, *Ambersons* set us dreaming again.

The Picture of Dorian Gray (1945) and
The Private Affairs of Bel Ami (1947). *Director-Writer:* Albert Lewin.
Stuffed to bursting with literary importance and almost painfully self-conscious about their pedigree, Lewin's films are not as serious as they mean to be, but more fun than they seem. *Dorian Gray* is a perfervid mounting of the Wilde tale, propelled by an odd combination of textual reverence, winningly over-the-top acting and static direction. Lewin always seemed leery of moving his camera, as if nothing should

detract from the primary importance of the plummy dialogue. But his movies resonate with keen melodramatic vigor. *Bel Ami*, from de Maupassant, is, the opening title announces, "the history of a scoundrel." Played by George Sanders—who else? who better?—this lowlife snakes his way through the salons and bedrooms of 1880 Paris. "My heart tells me that you're right," he tells one of his protesting paramours. "But I haven't listened to my heart for a long time." He romances the widow of his best friend while the pillow still shows the outline of the deceased's head; he puts the make on the wife of a blind musician at the very door of Notre Dame while the husband pumps away at the organ inside; he becomes, in short, the rage and preeminent rake of society...sort of a Julius Beaufort, with more artifice and even less scruple. In one memorable moment, this rogue reads a fervid declaration of love from one of his female admirers while shaving. As we hear her voice-over rising in furious declarations of passion, he wipes his razor on her billet-doux. High style.

THE SPIRAL STAIRCASE (1946) and THE STRANGE AFFAIR OF UNCLE HARRY (1945). *Director:* Robert Siodmak. *Writer of* Spiral: Mel Dinelli. *Writers of* Uncle Harry: Stephen Longstreet, Keith Winter.

Two more heady plunges into the dank Victorian psyche; film noir in period, but totally in character. *Uncle Harry* features George Sanders again, and poison, again. It suggests, with a nice undertow of humor, that the only way to find true love in such an ordered, arranged and muffled world is to murder for it. Hysteria is the keynote of *The Spiral Staircase*. The heroine is, literally, made mute by it, and by the ever-lurking presence of sexual violence. A conventional mystery in outline, Siodmak brings the story deeper into metaphor by using lots of German Expressionist chiaroscuro and some exquisite parlor tricks. At one point early on, he almost literally plunges into the killer's eye. Siodmak doesn't even bother with securing the polite veneer of middle-class Victorian America. This world, from the first, is a nightmare.

THE TOMB OF LIGEIA (1965). *Director:* Roger Corman. *Writer:* Robert Towne.

Lurid and loopy: degenerate romanticism carried past all reasonable extremities. But reasonable movies are no good at all. *The Tomb of Ligeia* amounts to a minor but hardy compulsion, having first appeared in the *Mean Streets*, where it stoked the fantasies of the neighborhood guys. This canny adaptation has little to do directly with Poe. Our Wharton rendering, by comparison, is a model of fidelity, a near transcription. But as Corman and Towne capture the deranged meter of Poe's malarial imagination, we hoped—and tried—to find a space we could comfortably inhabit within Wharton's orderly architecture. Maybe writing *Age* was not really a matter of adaptation, then. It was more a process of personalization, and then rediscovery. And, always, of learning lessons, and trying not to forget.

STILLS

Above: The Beaufort Ball begins.
Left: Winona Ryder, Daniel Day-Lewis.

Above: M.S., Daniel Day-Lewis, Winona Ryder.
Below: Mrs. Archer's Thanksgiving.

Farewell dinner for the Countess.

Above: Michael Ballhaus, M.S., Jay Cocks.
Below: Making 23rd Street, Manhattan, in Troy, N.Y.

Above: Miriam Margolyes as Mrs. Mingott.
Below: M.S. with Dante Ferretti, production designer.

141

Gabriella Pescucci, costume designer, and M.S.

Top: In the aviary: The Botanical Garden, the Bronx, N.Y.
Bottom: The social season with *Faust.*

143

CAST AND CREW CREDITS

COLUMBIA PICTURES presents

A Cappa/De Fina Production

A Martin Scorsese Picture

Daniel Day-Lewis   Michelle Pfeiffer   Winona Ryder

"THE AGE OF INNOCENCE"

Music by Elmer Bernstein   Director of Photography- Michael Ballhaus, A.S.C

Costume Designer- Gabriella Pescucci   Based upon the novel by Edith Wharton

Editor- Thelma Schoonmaker   Screenplay by Jay Cocks & Martin Scorsese

Production Designer- Dante Ferretti   Produced by Barbara De Fina

Directed by Martin Scorsese

CAST

Newland Archer	Daniel Day-Lewis
Ellen Olenska	Michelle Pfeiffer
May Welland	Winona Ryder

in order of appearance

Female Opera Singer	Linda Faye Farkas
Male Opera Singers	Michael Rees Davis
	Terry Cook
	Jon Garrison
Larry Lefferts	Richard E. Grant
Sillerton Jackson	Alec McGowen
Mrs. Welland	Geraldine Chaplin
Regina Beaufort	Mary Beth Hurt
Julius Beaufort	Stuart Wilson
Beaufort Guest	Howard Erskine
Party Guests	John McLoughlin
	Christopher Nilsson
Mrs. Mingott	Miriam Margolyes
Mrs. Archer	Siân Phillips
Janey Archer	Carolyn Farina
Henry van der Luyden	Michael Gough
Louisa van der Luyden	Alexis Smith
The Duke	Kevin Sanders
Mr. Urban Dagonet	W.B. Brydon
Gertrude Lefferts	Tracey Ellis
Countess Olenska's Maid	Cristina Pronzati
Florist	Clement Fowler
Mr. Letterblair	Norman Lloyd
Stage Actress	Cindy Katz
Stage Actor	Thomas Gibson
Zöe	As Herself
Rivière	Jonathan Pryce
Mingott Maid	June Squibb
Katie Blenker	Domenica Scorsese
Archer Maid	Mac Orange
Philip	Brian Davies
Archer Guest	Thomas Barbour
Bishop	Henry Fehren
Mary Archer	Patricia Dunnock
Ted Archer	Robert Sean Leonard

and

Joanne Woodward

as the narrator

CREW

Directed by	Martin Scorsese
Produced by	Barbara De Fina
Screenplay by	Jay Cocks &
	Martin Scorsese
Based upon the novel by	Edith Wharton
Director of Photography	Michael Ballhaus, A.S.C.
Production Designer	Dante Ferretti
Edited by	Thelma Schoonmaker
Costume Designer	Gabriella Pescucci
Music by	Elmer Bernstein
Title Sequence by	Elaine & Saul Bass
Co-Producer	Bruce S. Pustin
Associate Producer	Joseph Reidy
Casting by	Ellen Lewis
Unit Production Manager	Bruce S. Pustin
1st Assistant Director	Joseph Reidy
2nd Assistant Director	Joseph Burns
Art Director	Speed Hopkins
Assistant Art Directors	Dan Davis
	Robert Preziola
	Carl J. Sprague
Set Decorators	Robert J. Franco
	Amy Marshall
Key Set Dresser	Dave Weinman
Visual Research Consultant	Robin Standefer
Script Supervisor	Kathryn M. Chapin
Camera Operator	David M. Dunlap
First Assistant Camera	Florian Ballhaus
Second Assistant Camera	Bobby Mancuso
Steadicam Operators	Larry McConkey
	Anastos Michos
Assistant Production Manager & Location Manager	Patricia Anne Doherty
Assistant Costume Designer	George Potts
Production Mixer	Tod Maitlan
Boom Operator	J.T. O'Mara
Wardrobe Supervisors	Deirdre Nicola Williams
	Hartsell Taylor
Men's Wardrobe Attendant	Michael Adkins
Women's Wardrobe Attendant	Cheryl Kilbourne-Klimp
Makeup	Allen Weisinger
Special Effects Makeup	Manlio Rocchetti
Ms. Pfeiffer's Makeup	Ronnie Specter
Hair Design	Alan Dangerio

Hair Stylist	Michael Kriston
Hair Consultant	Antonio Soddu
Wigs by	Peter Owen
Chief Lighting Technician	Raymond Quinlan
Assistant Chief Lighting Technician	Jim Manzione
Key Grip	Dennis Gamiello
Second Grip	John Lowry
Dolly Grip	Brian Fitzsimmons
Chargeman Scenic Artist	James Sorice
2nd Second Assistant Director	Susan Fiore
Special Effects Coordinator	John Ottesen
Special Effects Operators	Ronnie Ottesen
	Mike Maggi
Animal Wranglers	Len Brooks
	Chris Sullivan
Production Coordinator	Alesandra M. Cuomo
Production Secretary	Katherine A. Kennedy
Production Accountant	Matilde P. Valera
Assistants to Mr. Scorsese	Margaret Bodde
	Heather Norton
Assistants to Ms. De Fina	Amy Henkels
	Wendy Sax
Assistant to Mr. Day-Lewis	Melissa Unger
Assistant to Ms. Pfeiffer	Amy Lynn
Assistant to Ms. Pescucci	Louise Lamanna
Art Department Coordinator	Michele Giordano
Property Master	James Mazzola
Assistant Property Master	Jeff Mazzola
Construction Coordinator	Ronald Petagna
Construction Grip	Vincent Guarriello
Transportation Captain	Michael Hyde
Transportation Co-Captain	Richard Holston
Casting Associate	Julie A. Madison
Dialect Coach	Tim Monich
First Assistant Film Editor	Alsia Lepselter
Second Assistant Film Editor	Joel R. Hirsch
Apprentice Film Editor	Yasmine Amitai
Supervising Sound Editor	Skip Lievsay
Dialogue Supervisor	Philip Stockton
Sound Effects Editor	Eugen Gearty
Foley Supervisor	Bruce Pross
ADR Editor	Hal Levinsohn
Dialogue Editors	Marissa Littlefield
	Laura Civiello
Re-Recording Mixer	Tom Fleischman
Music Editors	Suzana Perić
	Suki Buchman
Assistant Music Editor	Nic Ratner
Assistant Sound Editors	Sylvia Menno
	Chris Fielder
	Gina R. Alfaro
Foley Editors	Frank Kern
	Steve Visscher
19th Century Music Consultant	David Montgomery
Etiquette Consultant	Lili Lodge
Dramaturge	Michael X. Zelenak
Dance Consultant	Elizabeth Aldrich
Table Decoration Consultant	David McFadden
Chef 19th Century Meals	Rick Ellis
Catering	Coast to Coast Caterers
Extras Casting	Sylvia Fay
Extras Casting Associates	Fleet Emerson
	Deborah Rudy

Unit Publicist	Marion Billings
New York Location Assoc.	Joseph E. Iberti
	Michael Stricks
Still Photographer	Phillip V. Caruso
Troy Location Associate	Mark Von Holstein
Philadelphia Location Assoc.	Michael Nickodem
DGA Trainee	Mary Rae Thewlis
Art Department Assistants	Joanne Belonsky
	Tamara Malkin-Stuart
Production Assistants	John De Simone
	David Venghaus
	Julie Herrin
	Sara A. Thorson

PARIS CREW

Unit Production Manager	Jean-Pierre Avice
Unit Location Manager	Sandrine Ageorges
Second Assistant Director	Vincent Lascoumes
Art Director	Jean-Michel Hugon
Gaffer	Pierre Abraham
Key Grip	Charlie Freess
Production Coordinator	Joanny Carpentier
Unit Production Accountant	Christine Bodelot

Special Visual Effects by Illusion Arts, Inc.
Syd Dutton and Bill Taylor, A.S.C.

Matte Artist	Robert Stromberg
Matte Photography	Mark Sawicki
	John Sullivan
Optical Photography	David S. Williams, Jr.
Mechanical Effects	Lynn Ledgewood
Production Manager	Catherine Sudolcan

Soundtrack Available on Epic Soundtrax

Orchestration	Emilie Bernstein
Orchestra Contractor	Steven Danenberg

MUSIC

"Faust" (Opera)
Written by Charles F. Gounod

"Piano Sonata No. 8 in C Minor, Op. 13"
("Pathetique")
Written by Ludwig van Beethoven

"Radetzky March"
Written by Johann Strauss I
Performed by The Berlin Radio Symphony Orchestra
Courtesy of PolyGram Special Markets

"Emperor Waltz Op. 437"
Written by Johann Strauss II
Performed by The London Philharmonic
Courtesy of Collins Classics
By arrangement with Allegro

"Artist's Life"
Written by Johann Strauss II
Performed by Leonard Bernstein and the New York Philharmonic
Courtesy of Sony Classical

"Tales From The Vienna Woods"
Written by Johann Strauss II
Performed by The London Philharmonic
Courtesy of Collins Classics
By arrangement with Allegro

"Quintet In B Flat Op. 87, 3rd Movement"
Written by Felix Mendelssohn Bartholdy
Performed by Academy Chamber Ensemble
Courtesy of Philips Classics
By arrangement with PolyGram Special Markets

"Marble Halls"
Arranged by Enya, Roma Ryan and Nicky Ryan
Performed by Enya
Courtesy of Reprise Records and Warner Music U.K. Ltd.
By arrangement with Warner Special Products

Optical Effects by .... The Effects House
Post Production Facilities .... Sound One
Color Timer .... Mark Ginsberg
Negative Cutter .... T.A.B. Inc.
Shot in Super 35 Format with Arriflex 535

Prints by TECHNICOLOR®

Special Thanks to:

Furs provided by Fendi
Schumacher Fabrics
Crystal Items™ and © Baccarat 1992
Select Artwork Consultation by Christie's
Stationery provided by Tiffany & Co.
Costumes by Tirelli Costumi Roma and Barbara Matera Ltd. N.Y.

Costume Jewelry by Gioielli L.A.B.A. Roma
New York Historical Society
Ms. Letitia Baldridge

The Producers wish to thank the New York State Governor's Office
for Motion Picture and Television Development and the City of New York Mayor's Office of
Film, Theatre and Broadcasting for their extensive assistance, as well as the City of Troy.

With thanks to the City Hall of Paris
Remerciements à la Mairie de Paris

Stage Facilities by Kaufman Astoria Studios, New York